A FORTNIGHT IN AUGUST

A FORTNIGHT IN AUGUST

Martin Yeeles

Printed in the United States of America

First Printing, 2021

ISBN 978-0-981-6782-2-1

For my parents, brothers and sisters.

1.

Three and a half children.

'Wakey, wakey! Rise and shine!'

This is the girls' alarm call. Father crosses to the windows and pulls the curtains back with a flourish. The room is suddenly bathed in morning light. Next, he opens a window for fresh air, announcing the time in a loud voice as he leaves. The eldest daughter is the first to rise. The other two snooze for a little while longer. Once she has finished her ablutions, she goes straight from the bathroom to wake the boys. Father leaves it to her to get them up. It helps to stagger the use of the single bathroom. Her method is much gentler than her father's, creeping quietly between the bunk beds, slowly drawing back a sliver of a curtain to allow just a little light to seep in.

'Sorry boys,' she whispers, 'but it's quarter past seven. Time to get up.' She knocks on the door of the other bedroom and gets a grunt for a confirming response.

Breakfast is always a hectic, rushed affair. A large pot of tea is on the dining table, resting on a trivet and encased in a bright-red woollen tea cosy. There is a thermos of hot milk for cereal, a jug of cold milk for tea, a bowl of sugar, a fresh uncut loaf on a wooden board, yellow butter in a glass dish, jam and marmalade in their original jars. The children help themselves to boxes of cereal, plates, teacups, saucers and cutlery from the sideboard. Four slices of bread are grilled at a time on the eye-level gas burner, the potential for burning the toast means it is carefully watched. Breaking their fast in shifts, places at the table exchange rapidly. The radio is tuned to the news. After the headlines at the top of the hour, Father kisses Mother and calls goodbye to anyone within earshot. Gathering his work bag, he sets off on a brisk walk to the bus stop to catch the number forty-three into the town centre.

Within forty-five minutes of the parental alarm call, the house is cleared. Mother then sets to work on cleaning up the aftermath. The children are on their way to three different schools, by bus or by foot.

~~~

They live on a typical post-war housing estate; a government initiative to provide affordable housing for a growing population. Homes were allocated from a waiting list. The average family at the time consisted of three and a half children, so the semi-detached houses were built with three bedrooms. When Emily and Raymond found out that they had been selected for one of these new homes, they had just celebrated their one-year wedding anniversary, and they already had a newborn son, Kevin. The house was spacious compared to the flat that they had moved from. It had a fairly large garden in the back and a small yard in the front. There was a sitting room, a decent-sized kitchen with a separate dining room, and they did not even use the two extra bedrooms at first. They had decided that they both wanted a large family. Raymond, having been orphaned at a young age, was sent away to a boarding school, which separated him from the only other member of his family, his big sister. The loneliness that this created made him think at the time that, if he ever were to get married, he would want lots and lots of children, so that they would not feel the same isolation that he had experienced. They would always have each other.

Emily grew up with three other sisters and an older brother. Her father served in the army, so they lived on different bases around the world, moving often. But essentially, they were a normal Irish family from Dublin.

～～～

The common perception of good Irish Catholics having a lot of kids turned out to be true in this case. As Emily and Raymond's family grew, and grew up, they simply managed with what they had – eventually fitting nine children and two adults into a

small, three-bedroom, one-bathroom, semi-detached house;
Mother and Father sleeping on a pull-out bed in the living room.
Moving to a bigger house was not a financially viable option for
them. They simply made do.

2.
Hide and Seek.

Father rises as normal, but he does not disturb the children today. He has a solitary breakfast in the kitchen: toast with lashings of butter and strawberry jam, washed down with a mug of milky tea. He stands over the sink, looking out the window at his planted garden, listening to the news on Radio Four. He sets off quietly for work at the usual time.

⌇

The children are off school for the summer, which stretches deliciously before them. Six full weeks free of any structure. No set plans, just to be outside as much as possible. Nothing to do but play. Their much-anticipated holiday at the seaside is not until the final two weeks before they return to school, which makes it awkward for them in terms of how to handle their eagerness. They can hardly wait to be there. But they also do not want to wish away these lazy summer days, then be full of regret, wondering where it all went when they traipse back into school at the start of a new year.

On this first Monday morning, they have the luxury of lying in if they want to. Some do. But once they are all up and dressed and ready to face the day, they feel compelled to get out of the small house, eventually all of them gravitating towards the pavement and the strip of grass on the other side of their low, front-garden wall. It is the perfect dimension for a cricket wicket. The pavement that is, not the grassy area, which is too rutted and patchy for a true bounce. Although it is not quite the regulation-size length of twenty-two yards, when adjusted for a junior game with a tennis ball, then it is just right. They use an appropriately sized plank of found plywood to act as the stumps, propped up by a house brick on its end, and cracks in the pavement at either side become creases. The close proximity of the garden wall means that they only need fielders on the grassy strip side.

There is a climbable oak tree behind the 'wicket'; a rope attached to a stout branch for swinging, knotted at the other end around a smaller branch for a makeshift seat. Under its canopy is a small shallow pit, no more than six inches wide and three inches deep, which has been dug out for games of marbles. Mark is kicking a plastic football against the garden wall. Kathy is energetically skipping rope. The youngest boy, Martin, is belly-down in the grass, lining up some marbles for a lone practise game. Lorraine and Julie are sitting on the pavement behind the wicket, playing jacks: starting with onesies, then twosies, up until they can scoop all five of the little metal jacks before catching the rubber ball on the bounce. Kevin is twisting himself around on the swing, then letting it unravel, sending him a little dizzy, then doing it all over again. Peter is bowling slow, right-arm off-spin to David, who blocks the deliveries with textbook forward defensive strokes, fielding his own shots to return the ball to the bowler.

Kevin plants his feet on the ground to steady himself and looks around at his spinning siblings.

'How about a game of kick-the-ball-hide-and-seek?' he suggests once he has gathered himself. A family favourite pastime, the idea is well received. As they cluster together, Kevin determines who will be the seeker by chanting a familiar rhyme, pointing to each of them in turn on every syllable.

> *Eeny, meeny, miny, moe,*
> *Catch a tiger by the toe.*
> *If he screams, let him go,*
> *Eeny, meeny, miny, moe.*

On the last syllable he lands on Kathy. In a conventional game of hide-and-seek, the seeker closes their eyes and counts to one hundred while the others find hiding places. But in their kick-the-ball version, the retrieval of the kicked ball determines the amount of time to hide. The seeker must place the ball back at home base before she can go and find them. The hiders either stay as quiet as possible until they are found or try to run back to 'home' without being detected to kick the ball away, which releases anyone who has been captured.

Mark is designated as the kicker and they prepare to start the game, each of them scoping the landscape for favourable hiding spots. He places the ball carefully, much like a goalkeeper about to take a goal kick. He takes five steps back, then runs up to thump the ball high and long, grunting with the effort on impact.

'Wow!' Kathy is in awe, before realizing she has to go and fetch it. Everyone scatters. Julie keeps it simple and tucks in behind the oak tree. When Kathy returns with the ball under her arm, she immediately notices Julie's feet poking out from behind the trunk.

'One, two, three no erky. Julie behind the tree!'

Julie skulks out from her hiding place and stands near the placed ball, arms folded, as Kathy goes in search of the others. David has reached the furthest, heading quickly in the opposite direction of the kicked ball, finding a scalable tree and climbing up into its branches. He feels safe in the knowledge that the seeker would be foolish to come so far away from home. If they left the football exposed, even if he was spotted, he might outsprint them back. This is his usual tactic, one which wins him many games. The first one found is the next seeker, and the last is the winner. It also means that he rarely gets found. Which is how it turns out today. Kathy has eventually gathered all of them, apart from David, and they wait by the ball in a loose huddle. She is wary that he could appear at any moment to kick the ball away and free them, so is not venturing too far. Peter has sat down, his back against the tree trunk. Bored now. It has been going on too long. Lorraine also sits down on the pavement and pulls the five jacks and rubber ball from her pocket and starts playing again. Mark is expertly keeping the football away from Martin. He's tormenting him by rolling the ball close, then pulling it away with the sole of his foot. Martin tries to attack from different angles, but always fails. Julie is picking un-pillaged blackberries from the hedge that separates them from the road, popping them into her mouth. Kevin drifts off, going inside to get a drink of water. Kathy assesses the situation, hands on hips. She cannot waste time out here. She has things to do. Correspondence to take care of. So, she calls the game off with a lusty shout of surrender.

'Olly olly oxen free!'

David, high up and comfortable in the branches of a tree, cocks his head to pick up on the distant call, then pumps his fist.

'Yes!' he says to himself and begins to climb down.

3.
Pen Pals.

The family do not have a telephone installed in the house, which makes it difficult for Kathy to keep in touch with her friends. Rather than make use of the public telephone down the road by the shops, she prefers to write to them. She and her pen pals are equally satisfied with this back and forth, enjoying the conventionality and the eager anticipation of a reply.

Monday, July 17, 1972.

Dear Mary,
How are you?
Aren't you glad that school is over? I am. I need a break from all that Latin and Chemistry! My eldest brother, Kevin wouldn't even help me! He said I should figure it out for myself. I suppose he's right. Arrgghh! He did Physics and Applied Mathematics

11

for his A levels so I don't know what help he would be anyway!

I am really looking forward to seeing you and all your brothers and sisters again! The little ones have probably all grown a lot since last summer. We won't be getting there until Saturday the twelfth. A whole month away!

When are you getting there?

Are all the family coming this year?

Kathy.

P.S. Lorraine is teaching me how to play the guitar, maybe we can play some songs together?!!

~~~

Friday, July 22

Dear Kathy,

Lovely to hear from you as always, and yes, I am sooooo happy to not be in school too!

We will be driving down tomorrow (Saturday). It takes us about five hours to get from Wallingford to Cornwall. I'm not looking forward to the journey as it's always cramped and uncomfortable with all of us together with our belongings. Yes, we are all coming! I wish we lived as close as you do!

I'm excited to hear that you are playing guitar! We can definitely plan on some duets! We have been making up silly songs to entertain the youngest ones, so that could be fun too.

You can send a reply to Mrs. Bellamy's. We go there most days. See you in a few weeks!

Mary

~~~

Wednesday, August 2

Mary Lane
c/o Bellamy's Cafe,
Cliff Road,
Whitsand Bay,
Cornwall

Dear Mary,
Well, time is flying by!
I'm sure you are enjoying the beach ... I'm so jealous.
Everyone has settled into their summer here – Julie
has learned how to hula-hoop! She's really good at
it. The boys just play football or cricket all day long,
apart from Kevin, he stays in his room listening to
his noisy records – what a dirge!
I've been helping out at St. Joe's most days, I can tell
you all about that when we see each other.
This year, we are all going together in a twelve-seater
van that will pick us up in the morning and drive
us straight to Whitsands. What a luxury. No more
ferries and buses! Hurrah!
Can't wait!!!

Kathy

~~~

Friday, August 4

Dear Christine,
I hope you are enjoying your summer so far. Isn't it
nice not to be in class? Are you still planning on coming to see me at Whitsands for the day on Saturday,
the nineteenth? Will you talk to Yvonne and Natalie
to remind them? I imagine you will be planning it
together ... I wish we had a telephone at home like
you all do, everything would be so much easier!
You will see that I have enclosed the bus timetable
from the Torpoint side of the ferry. It's important

that you get there early because they run every thirty minutes on the hour and half hour only until ten o'clock, and then just on the hour after that. Please try and get at least the nine o'clock bus so that you can spend as much of the day here as possible. Let me know if that will be your plan. I can meet you at the top of the cliff and we can walk down together (ask the driver to tell you when you reach Freathy, that's our beach). Hopefully it won't be raining! Also you should probably aim to get the five o'clock bus back to the ferry rather than the six o'clock because by the time you get off the ferry in Devonport it would already be getting late and you still have two buses to catch to get home.

Sorry if I sound bossy!

Can't wait to see you!

Kathy

〰

The distinctive sound of the letter-slot flap being pushed open and quickly released to snap shut causes Kathy to drop her slice of buttered toast onto her plate and rush from the dining room, through the kitchen and into the hallway. One letter and a postcard are lying on the mat. Julie is right behind her.

'Is it?' Julie is excited.

'Nope. They're both for me.'

Julie trudges off, realizing that was her last chance of getting her O level results before their holiday. She wishes that they had come today; now she will just be anxious about it the whole fortnight.

Kathy returns to her breakfast. As she takes a bite of toast, she holds up the postcard in her other hand and studies the picture of a familiar coastline, then flips it over.

> Dear Kathy,
> Wish you were here. Oh, you will be! The weather has
> been awful – please bring the sunshine with you...
>
> Mary

She wipes her knife on the side of her plate and uses it to open the envelope.

> Dear Kathy,
> Thanks for your letter and the very useful bus time-
> table! We will definitely be on the nine o'clock bus
> next Saturday. I spoke to Natalie on the telephone
> yesterday and she said that her Dad has offered to
> bring Yvonne and I from home and drop us off at the
> ferry in the morning, and he is also going to pick us
> up on the way home at about quarter to six. How
> nice! Although why couldn't he just take us all the
> way to Whitsands!? Just kidding!
> Yes, I hope it won't be raining too! I want to lie on
> the beach all day and go swimming!
> See you Saturday,
>
> Christine

~~~

After breakfast, Kathy has one more letter to write.

> Friday, August 11
>
> Dear Christine,
> If your plans change for any reason you can write
> to me at this address:
>
> c/o Mrs. Bellamy's Cafe,
> Cliff Road,
> Whitsand Bay,
> Cornwall.

Otherwise, I will meet you as arranged from the nine o'clock Torpoint bus.

Kathy

~~~

After reviewing the businesslike letter, she folds it into thirds and places it within the envelope, and then adds the address to it. Next, she locates a first-class stamp from the drawer within the bureau in the living room, licks the back of it, then applies it to the top right-hand corner of the envelope. She also licks the adhesive strip to seal it, the unpleasant taste making her wrinkle her nose.

Before heading to the postbox, she looks for her mother to see if she needs any last-minute shopping doing while she is out.

Kathy is often enlisted to go over the mealtime plans. At fourteen years old, she is the best shopper in the family, knows all the prices by heart. She has taken Cookery classes at school, where she not only learned how to make home-cooked food – like Swiss rolls, apple crumble, Scotch eggs, and even exotic dishes such as prawn cocktail – but she was also taught how to spend wisely and make the most judicious use of available funds.

~~~

A week before, thoughts had turned towards practicalities in preparation for the trip. To save money – and by shopping in the local supermarket, rather than relying on an isolated village shop for their provisions – they would bring as much non-perishable food with them as they could. Mother and Kathy settled down together at the dining table after the tea-time dishes had been cleared away, to go over a menu plan for the first week of the holiday.

Mother had said to her, 'You know what it's like there, Kathy. And I don't want to spend all my holiday thinking about food, or shopping for groceries and ending up in the kitchen all day.'

Kathy shares her plan.

'OK. Here's what I was thinking. Saturday, we'll be settling in, so let's keep it simple. Beans on toast. Angel Delight for pudding.' Kathy recites from the notes that she has prepared in her notebook.

Mother had an existing list, already quite substantial, with staples such as milk, eggs and flour, as well as canned goods for sandwiches and sweet things. She adds Mother's Pride, thick slice times two; Beans times four; then adds Angel Delight times two, then a dash.

'Butterscotch?' Kathy nods. Everyone loves butterscotch, so Mother adds 'butterscotch' after the dash.

'Sunday, following Mass, we can pick up pasties from the bakery, then for tea we can do crumpets, with Battenberg for afters?'

Mother adds 'Crumpets times two' and 'Battenberg'.

'We can also pick up some extra stuff from the Co-op there at the same time: beetroot, tomatoes, maybe boil some eggs for a salad on Monday?'

'Especially if it's sunny, salad would be lovely. Oh, I'll need some salad cream.' She adds it to the list.

'Fishcakes and chips?'

'Good idea.' Mother adds 'Salmon, four cans'.

'Wednesday...'

Mother has a suggestion. 'How about cauliflower cheese? We could get a couple of cauliflowers at Millbrook too on the Sunday.'

Kathy agrees; Mother adds 'Cheddar' to the list.

For Thursday they decide on a beef stew with dumplings for tea – something they can prepare early in the day and let it cook slowly – while Mother will make a family favourite for pudding: lemon meringue pie. Although she is not promising it if the weather is nice.

Rather than stick with their usual Friday fish meal of haddock, mashed potato, peas and a white parsley sauce, to keep the prep time short they will go with fish fingers and chips to end the week. They already have a ten-pound bag of potatoes in the pantry, and they can buy the fish fingers while they are there. They agree to send a couple of the boys up to the bigger supermarket at Whitleigh Green. They will need the extra-large shopping trolley.

~~~

Today, she finds Mother in the living room, hunched over her sewing machine. As usual, Kathy asks her if she needs anything while she is out.

'Well, maybe we should do something special tonight, don't you think?' suggests Mother.

Kathy agrees. The night before they left home was almost

the best night of the holiday, although it was spent at home and the sea was still as far away as ever. The level of excitement and anticipation bettered only by Christmas Eve.

'So, I was thinking toad-in-the-hole?'

'Mmmm, lovely! Dad's favourite. A dozen sausages?'

Mother nods. 'And a cabbage.'

'Afters?'

'I'll make a trifle.' She is delighted with herself. Not just for the idea, but that she can make this dessert without a recipe, using ingredients that they already have in the pantry and fridge.

4.
Holiday Eve.

The office was behind Father now. Once he stepped onto the bus home, he really did feel that the holiday had already begun. It was the precise moment when any last thoughts of his work were dissolved, and the next fortnight stretched wonderfully ahead.

He was often greeted by some of his children, waiting for his arrival at the bus stop so that they could accompany him on the short walk home. And today of all days he was expecting a good showing. They would be excited if he was carrying an extra bag, keen to inspect its contents. It was usually just vegetables, fruit or meat from the market in town, but sometimes he picked up five-pound bags of broken biscuits from Woolworths. These were seconds that had been damaged in transit; perhaps a wholesale box had been dropped, rendering a layer of packets unsellable. Most of these biscuits were still in pristine condition, but the policy of the store was to empty the entire packet into a clear plastic bag, the process continuing until it was filled with a random assortment: Custard Creams, Malted Milks, Rich Tea, Pink Wafers, Nice, Ginger Nuts, Chocolate Bourbon, Shortbread, Fig Rolls. Then the bag would be sealed and placed for discounted sale at the back corner of the store, along with expiring perishable items.

As the bus slows for his stop, Father stands ready at the exit door and looks ahead. Sure enough, Kevin, Peter, David, Martin and Julie are right there. As soon as Father alights David takes his workbag from him and swings it about purposefully, pretending that he is the one who has just returned from the office. Martin immediately takes his free hand. Peter takes his other bag from him.

'Broken biscuits!' he yells, his best hope confirmed.

Julie skips around him, showing off a new haircut from many angles.

~~~

This nightly display did not go unnoticed by his fellow passengers. The regulars would look forward to this daily greeting too, looking up from their daily newspapers or craning their necks to see if he was on their bus today as his stop approached. Bill Rogers usually caught the same bus home as Father. They did not know each other by name, the most they ever acknowledged was a nod, or a goodnight, but they both alighted at the same stop on Budshead Road. Bill preferred to sit downstairs, so they only saw each other as they gathered at the exit door. He assumed that they must work similar hours. Often the first thing he would say to his wife as he came in the door was the daily headcount.

'There were five of 'em tonight.'

'Five of who?'

'Them kids. At the bus stop. The poor fella that gets off the same stop as me. All these blimmin' kids, they're all over 'im as soon as 'e steps off the bus.'

'Awww, I think it's lovely.'

~~~

The children each have their own set place at the dining table. Three on each long side, two at each end, in a boy–girl–boy–girl arrangement. It is a tight fit; all the more intimate this evening as they chatter excitedly with anticipation. Over the clatter of knives and forks on plates, Mother and Father are fussing over practicalities: instructing them about packing their bags and being ready on time in the morning. The children dream about long hours of cricket in the baking sun, and invigorating plunges in the sea. As they bustle about clearing away their dirty dishes, Julie is inspired to start singing an appropriate and infectious pop song: Cliff Richard's 'Summer Holiday'. They all know the words and join in immediately, grinning at each other:

We're all going on a summer holiday,
No more working for a week or two.

Fun and laughter on our summer holiday,
No more worries for me or you.
For a week or two.

We're going where the sun shines brightly.
We're going where the sea is blue.
We've seen it in the movies,
Now let's see if it's true.

~~~

After tea, in what has now become something of a tradition the evening before their holiday, Father lines up the three youngest boys for haircuts.

Normally, he gives each of them a variation of the classic crew cut. Military style. Like Elvis when he joined up. The sides and back are cut as for a regular crew cut, but then the top is cut a longer length, about half an inch over the top, what he refers to as a Classic Taper. He leaves the hair long enough to run a comb through it, with a parting option, and gradually tapers it down short around the ears and the neck. He is proud of his handiwork. Every Sunday he would line each of them up for inspection before going to church, wetting the comb in the sink then running it through their hair to get the parting well defined, then smoothing their eyebrows with a damp thumb. The boys looked sharp.

But for Whitsands, they get a no-nonsense buzz cut.

Father goes into a reverie as he runs the clippers around David's nape.

I'd make a good barber, he thinks to himself.

Not just because he knows how to cut hair. He is a people person. He would make them feel better about themselves. They would leave his chair happier than when they came in. Not just because of the haircut and the raising of self-esteem that comes from a new look, but he would engage them in conversation. Find out their story. Get them chatting about themselves.

~~~

Father steps around to continue with the right side of David's haircut, pulling on the boy's ear with his thumb and forefinger to make access easier. He could learn the trade in his spare time. Go part-time at first. Saturdays. That is probably the busiest day for a barber anyway. He wonders what they get paid, how it works. *Are they employed? Or do they work independently, perhaps keeping what they earn directly from the customer and paying a percentage to the boss. Do they get good tips?* He imagines he would need to build up a client base, regulars who would keep coming back to him. He could check out that place above Jon Conway's in town, near his workplace. They always seem busy. He could go in for a haircut on his lunch break, see how it all works, ask questions.

'Ow!' David whines as Father gets a little heavy-handed negotiating the clippers around the sensitive bone near the back of his right ear. That snaps Father out of his musings. What is he thinking? He is never going to leave the Gas Board. He has been there twenty-five years already. He will get a good pension eventually. The steady income. The familiarity with his role. The job security. He is not about to change career on a whim. Not with all these mouths to feed. He finishes up around the crown and top, then runs a rough hand over David's hair, dislodging all the loose freshly cut strands of hair. He then whips the nylon cape away from around the boy's shoulders.

'Next!'

The boys all feel that the haircuts their father gives them are too short, especially this Whitsands variety. They laugh and point as each emerges from the chair, despite the fact that they get the same cut in the end. They are just thankful that they will not be ridiculed in school on Monday morning.

'It'll grow back.' Not exactly a ringing endorsement from an aspiring barber.

〰

That afternoon, Mother had taken the two oldest girls on the bus to the hairdressers in town for bob cuts. They were both happy to have this medium-length style with a fringe at the front. Father would cut their hair too when they were younger. He gave them bowl cuts, literally sticking an appropriately sized bowl on their heads and removing all the hair left exposed below. This was a style that had become common in the Depression era of the thirties because it was an easy haircut to do at home. The two older boys received these haircuts too, until they both objected that they looked the same as each other. Kathy was the first to rebel, insisting on growing her hair out longer so as not to resemble her brother, Mark. She would brush her hair regularly under the belief that it would help it grow faster.

~~~

Despite the boys' objections, the severe haircuts signify that their annual holiday is imminent. The anticipation is palpable. All that is left to do is to pack.

5.
Run-Ragged, part one.

Mother rarely threw away any of the children's clothes during the year. She would often spend an evening in her sitting room chair by the gas fire darning socks or holes in jumpers, replacing broken zips or lost buttons. She would also buy fabric to make dresses and wool to knit jumpers, using patterns that were either loaned from the library or were included in her *Woman's Own* magazine. The boys and girls were used to being asked to stand up with arms stretched wide for measurements during an evening in front of the television. As Mother would run the tape measure around waists, chests and along arms, the child would usually be looking beyond her, eyes still fixed on the screen. One time she read the measurement of the youngest's waist from the wrong side of the tape ('Forty-six! That can't be right, Martin'), standing back with her hand on his shoulder, looking at his tiny waist then back at her tape before realizing the mistake. Mark tried to establish 'Forty-six' as a new nickname, but it never stuck.

Aside from the two eldest children, Kevin and Lorraine, all of the children's clothes and shoes are handed-down as they are outgrown or home-made. If an item is deemed too far gone to be presentable – say, a T-shirt that has lost its shape over numerous washes, or a big toe is suddenly protruding through a plimsoll – then it is to be reserved in a pile for one final fling: what she calls 'run-ragged at Whitsands.' These pieces are on their last legs, no amount of sewing or patching will save them. They have served the family well over the years.

~~~

She goes through the run-ragged pile, making the final repairs to see them last the next two weeks.

'There you go Peter,' she flings his favourite brown zip-up cardigan across the room to him, 'good as new.'

Peter admires the freshly applied tan-coloured leather elbow patches and decides that this would be a good time to pack.

'None of your nice stuff, Peter,' Mother reminds him, 'it's run-ragged. Okay?'

He heads upstairs to his bedroom and begins to lay out the clothes he will wear at the seaside. He is not planning on bringing many clothes with him. In fact, he reckons that they should all fit into his green-and-white Plymouth Argyle holdall. At Mother's

30

suggestion, he will leave behind his Ben Sherman button-down collar shirts, both the red and the navy blue one; he only bought them from the Littlewoods catalogue with his birthday money in January, so they are staying home. However, he does decide to pack his Brutus penny-rounder in bottle green and an older blue-and-white-checked short-sleeve shirt. He stuffs in two more jumpers: a blue one with a stitched picture of a bird and clouds on it, and a white ribbed pullover with black trimming on the cuffs and collar. He throws in a couple of T-shirts, long and short pants from the bottom of the drawer, a pair of swimming trunks, underwear, and socks. A pair of Dunlop Green Flash tennis shoes and his recently inherited pair of plastic red jelly buckled sandals squash in on top of his clothes. He zips up the holdall by pinching together the sides of the bag with one hand and forcing the slider along the teeth with the other. Stepping back to admire his efficiency, Peter is ready for his holiday.

〜

There were a few favourite items of clothing whose history could be traced through family photographs. Often the children would look through the albums together, pointing and giggling at each other, or asking their parents to explain who the people were in black and white.

That evening, Kathy and David are sat at the dining table, initially to review past holiday photographs, anticipating the new memories to be made this year. Mother has seen an opportunity for them to update the latest album, and hands them a shoebox filled with loose packs of recent photographs. They are trusted to make the edits: which pictures are worthy, which ones belong on the same spread, and following some loose chronological order. Kathy opens up an older album and comes across a photograph of herself and her two sisters, presumably taken a few years previously judging by their looks. They are lined up on the stoop of the house, outside the front door, a favourite spot of Father's for documenting the family for some reason. All are smiling. Kathy notices that she looks a little shy – her hand reaching up to her face, one knee coyly bent, she is turned sideways towards her sisters. Then she notices something else. Lorraine's dress. It is a pretty white frock buttoned up the front, with short sleeves, and with a collar that is embroidered with flowers.

'That's my dress.'

David glances over at the picture that she has her finger on.

'That's Julie's dress.'

Returning to his own pile of pictures, he comes across a group picture also taken in the front garden. They are all there, apart from Kevin. He remembers the day well. Their Aunty and Uncle were visiting from Canada, so they were all excited. He studies the photograph. Most of them are squinting into the sun and smiling. His brother Mark is slightly hidden in the back row, tilting his head to be visible from behind his sister. Only his head and shoulders are seen. Now it is David's turn to notice something. Mark is wearing a very distinctive rust-coloured, cable-knit sweater.

'That's my jumper!'

Kathy leans in to look, then guffaws. 'You're wearing it!'

He had not even realized that he was wearing the same jumper at that moment.

~~~

The best clothes were cherished, they would not be needed at Whitsands; but for a fortnight in August the run-ragged pile was perfect. The children could scramble on the rocks, roll in the grass of the cottage's garden, throw layers into the sand when they got too hot, or use jumpers for goalposts. It did not matter if they ruined them. Most of these items would not be coming back home with them to Plymouth anyway.

6.
All the Things.

The two youngest boys, David and Martin, are walking
back from the sweet shop when the distinctive yellow passenger
van passes them. They knew that it was on its way, but they
are far too excited to sit at home and wait. Besides, they need
to stock up on supplies. On the way to the shop, they play their
usual game of 'Next Lamppost'. Once the challenge had been
set by one of them by calling out 'Next lamppost!' they would
sprint to reach it first. The starting point was always the lamppost they were passing, so they were aware that a declaration
could be issued by either of them at any time. The older brother,
David, is bigger and stronger so always wins, despite Martin's
strenuous efforts. Martin would either be beaten by a well-
timed late surge, or be held off contemptuously, being casually

observed as he struggled to keep pace. David imagines himself as the top racehorse jockey at the time, Lester Piggott, adopting his intimidating winning style. One time, Martin had caught his brother by surprise by distracting him with the old trick of pointing to the side and saying, 'Look over there!' then shouting out the challenge over his shoulder, already ten paces ahead. No 'on you marks' or 'get set' about it. He was off. His brother rallied and was level with him as they crossed the imaginary line, Lester Piggott brandishing his whip. Out of breath from the effort, and laughing at his own audacity, Martin declared himself the winner. This was disputed. Surely it was a dead heat?

'But if it was a photo finish I would have won, right?'

David generously conceded. Just this once.

~~~

They do not race on the return from the shop, they are busy enjoying their Tip Tops: long clear plastic tubes filled with frozen juice. In their paper bags they have Sherbet Fountains, Smarties, Black Jacks, Rolos, plus a couple of bars of Caramac for the journey. As the van passes them, they quickly finish their Tip Tops and excitedly pick up the pace. Fast walking at first, then breaking into a steady jog, matching strides side by side, much like long distance runners. They are already at the pink path, which leads to the new housing estate behind their family home, so they know they are only about a minute or so away. The van would be turning onto Milford Lane by now, probably performing the required three-point turn, pulling up on the near side of the street, ready to load up. As the boys reach the garden gate, they look for the parked van and hear the unmistakable mechanical clicking of a handbrake being applied. They burst into the kitchen to announce its arrival.

'It's here!' they call to the house.

Everything is lined up and ready in the hallway: a pile of suitcases and holdalls stuffed full of summer clothes, hats, sandals, towels and toiletries, a plastic football, a cricket bat, stumps and bails, tennis balls, badminton racquets and a couple of shuttlecocks, Julie's hula hoop, a pile of library books and assorted comics and magazines.

And then there is the food: wooden crates and plastic carrier bags filled with bottles of milk, cartons of eggs and bags of flour. There are multiple cans of Spam, sardines, pilchards, tuna fish, salmon and Fray Bentos corned beef. Tins of Heinz baked beans, tomato soup, spaghetti hoops and salad cream. Ambrosia rice pudding and mixed fruits in syrup. There are jars of Marmite, Robinson's marmalade and lemon curd. Shallow jars of Shippams salmon fish paste. Sachets of Angel Delight. Packs of Jell-O. Loaves of Mother's Pride sliced white bread. Packets of crumpets. Three bottles of Robinson's undiluted orange squash, two bottles of Ribena. A jumbo box of Tetley tea bags. Jars of Cadbury's drinking chocolate and Horlicks. A two-pound bag of Tate and Lyle white sugar. Columns of Rich Tea and Digestive biscuits. Two rectangular packs of Jacob's cream crackers. A McVitie's Jamaica ginger cake, a Battenberg cake, a couple of boxed trays of Mr Kipling's cherry and almond bakewell tarts. Several packs of Penguin chocolate biscuits. Boxes of Tunnock's tea cakes. A huge block of cheddar cheese. A stack of half a dozen carton wheels of Dairylea soft cheese triangles. Bulky but lightweight boxes of Kellogg's Rice Krispies and Cornflakes. Weetabix, Ready Brek and Farley's Rusks. Then runner beans, protruding sticks of rhubarb, beetroot, cucumbers, heads of lettuce and potatoes picked from the garden.

All the things that a family of ten would need for two weeks at the seaside.

～～

'Knock, knock!'

With an announcement rather than an actual knock on the back door, a short, bespectacled, grey-haired lady bustles straight into the kitchen, an old biscuit tin in her hand.

'It's only me.'

She immediately notices all the luggage and provisions stacked up in the hallway. 'Oh! Are you all ready to go, like?' She turns back from the hallway to see David entering the kitchen and standing next to his mother.

'Oh 'eavens!' She rocks back on her heels to take him all in, hands clasped in front of her around the tin, a handbag hanging from one elbow. 'Look how tall you're getting. You'll be bigger than me soon!'

She is only four feet ten, so David really hopes that to be true. She is a regular visitor, but usually the children are all in school when she comes by. She turns her attention back to Mother.

'I'm glad I caught you, I was just popping by to see if you needed anything done, like. You know, while you're away.'

~~~

People would often ask Mother how she could possibly manage with so many children. Some would ask it with admiration. Others were horrified. Some, as they watched the family traipse by, wondered *How does she even keep track of who is who?* In truth, Martin in particular was accustomed to being called by all his brothers' names before his own.

'Oh, Kevin. I mean, Mark. No, Peter, David. Sorry, Martin! Martin, that's the fella! Would you fetch me some parsley from the garden, just a handful.'

She is a housewife. She has chosen to devote all her time, energy and love into creating a safe, warm, clean home for her family to grow and thrive. She cooks and cleans. It seems like she is constantly washing clothes, all by hand, then lugging the damp laundry in a huge basket and a bag of clothes pegs to hang them up to dry in the back garden, using a pulley system similar to lowering then raising a really heavy flag. Or she is bent over her Singer sewing machine mending them. She plans every meal. Shops for groceries with extremely careful money management. Sometimes the older children would act as the younger children's caretakers, or they would help out with errands, and she was always quick to say that she did not do it all alone. So, when she was asked, 'How do you manage?' she was always ready with a specific answer.

'Mrs Fryer.'

The children do not even know her first name; the formality does not mean that she is aloof. They have always known her as Mrs Fryer. It is more of a sign of respect than anything. Like a favourite schoolteacher. She is loved by all of them.

Originally from Tenby in Wales, Mrs Fryer lives next door with her dour husband, Jim. They are childless, which may account for her interest in helping out the large family. Every Monday morning without fail, after the children leave for school, she shows up to help with the chores. Her first task is to strip all the beds and give them to Mother for washing. While that is underway, she fills a bucket with hot soapy water and goes around the house mopping the floors, then vacuuming the carpets. By the time she returns to the kitchen, Mother is squeezing the wet laundry through the wringer, turning the crank furiously, while Mrs Fryer gathers the bedding in the laundry basket, which she then takes out to the back garden to hang out to dry.

Then they have a break and a chat. Usually over a cup of tea and a sandwich, which is the only form of compensation that Mrs Fryer will accept for her hard work. By the time they catch up with their news and finish their refreshment, everything on the line is usually dry. Her final task is to make all the beds. If she was going shopping for groceries, she would often pop in to see if Mother needed anything, 'While I'm out, like.' When Mother was in the hospital giving birth, it was Mrs Fryer who took care of the children at home. First one child, then two. Then three. Then four, five, six, seven, eight. She would always remember the children's birthdays with hand-delivered cards, Sellotaping a half-crown inside and writing: "Happy birthday. From Mrs Fryer & Jim."

~~~

Mother assures her that there is nothing for her to worry about while they are away, so Mrs Fryer turns to leave, wishing them to have a nice time, adding her usual goodbye.

'Well, I must be off.'

Then she realizes that she still has the cake tin.

'I almost forgot. I made some Welsh cakes for you all, see? I know Kathy likes 'em.'

Mother thanks her for her thoughtfulness.

'Okay. There we are then,' she summarizes before leaving.

Mother adds the cake tin to the end of the pile in the hallway, just as the first bags at the other end are taken away.

7.

Helen.

It takes half an hour to load the van, and a further ten minutes for Mother to get everyone situated and buckled in. Father uses this time for a final check on the house. Windows are shut tight. Any electrical appliances are unplugged. All lights are switched off. Taps are turned tightly. Sink plugs are corked in place. He unfurls the bath plug chain from around the cold tap and fits it into the drain-hole. All food is removed from the refrigerator, perishables from the pantry too. He makes sure all the internal doors are closed over, then he locks the back door with a big key and a bolt from the inside. Before crossing the threshold of the front door, he glances back in the hallway one last time, then closes the door shut behind him. Rubbish is already in the dustbins ready for collection on Wednesday.

The morning paper has been stopped. The milkman has been informed to halt deliveries for the next two weeks. Finally, he goes around the side of the house to make sure that the padlock is in place on the garden shed – a chore he had taken care of the evening before, but he still feels compelled to rattle the lock to confirm it remains secure. He considers unlocking the front door to glance in once again, but stops himself, realizing that it really is not necessary, while also wary of the vanload of people waiting for him.

Walking around the van to take his spot in the passenger seat, he glances in at his family. He pulls open the door; but, before he commits, he leans in, resting his hand on the top of the seatback to check that the children are all present and correct. There are five boys and three girls. The youngest is eight, the eldest about to turn eighteen. Kevin, Lorraine, Julie, Mark, Kathy, Peter, David, Martin ...

There is one missing.

~~~

Helen was born two years after Martin. Her short life was a struggle from the start. A heart defect was detected early on and she was never able to fully develop, passing away after just three difficult years. Mother and Father took her to the hospital when her condition had deteriorated. A doctor approached them as they sat in the waiting room to tell them that they were sorry to inform them that there was nothing they could do for her and that their youngest daughter had died. Despite the pair of them feeling inconsolable, they had no other choice but to leave the hospital to catch the next bus home and simply carry on. Apart from the funeral, there was no grieving period. Mother busied herself with taking care of the other children and Father went back to work. The younger members of the family were not really old enough for Helen's passing to fully understand it, whereas, for the older children, it was deeply saddening. Father in particular struggled with her loss. For weeks, rather than catch his usual bus home from work he would take long walks, eventually ending up at home. No one knew where he was during these hours, and they would all wait anxiously for his return.

The reason that they were able to have a holiday at all was a direct result of this tragedy. The bungalow where they were to stay was owned by Father's boss, Mr Symons. After a few months of seeing him depressed at work, not his usual self, Mr Symons granted him a compassionate leave of absence, suggesting that the family take a break by staying at his seaside cottage, free of charge. He drove them there in his car the first time, which took two trips. He picked them up again after the fortnight; although, so that he would not need to make a second journey, Mother and some of the older children made an adventure of it. Waving the others off at the top of the cliff, they waited for the bus to the nearby village of Cawsand. From there, they took the small passenger ferry boat straight off the beach at high tide, around the scenic Rame peninsula to the Barbican in Plymouth. A walk into the city centre, then a final bus home, arriving a couple of hours later than the rest of the family.

~~~

On the car ride home, Mr Symons could see how much good the holiday had done them all. The children excitedly told him stories of playing in the surf, building sandcastles and climbing on the rocks. Even Father described the lovely clifftop walks and sunning himself on the beach without a care in the world. He borrowed one of his mother-in-law's expressions.

'Nothing to do and all day to do it.'

Mr Symons was so moved that, there and then, in the car, he announced to them that they could go back every year from now on, for the same two weeks in August. Father could not believe his luck, asking him over and over again if he meant it.

'Wait till we tell your mother!' he said, facing the children all squashed together in the back seat.

Mr Symons would say that he gained as much satisfaction from this act of generosity as they did from being the recipients of it. They would not have been able to afford it otherwise; on Father's salary there was not any room for frivolous luxuries like a fortnight's holiday at the seaside. Although he insisted on paying something, so they finally agreed on a heavily discounted rate.

So, Helen was often in their collective minds; especially at Whitsands, a place that she was never able to experience herself. Martin would subsequently be introduced as the baby of the family, which he never really accepted. Apart from objecting to being referred to as a baby, when he clearly was not one anymore, he felt that it was not true. That was still Helen.

~~~

Father takes his place next to the driver, who gives him a nod before turning to his passengers to make sure they are all ready to go. He is met with a sea of shiny, smiling faces.

'Are we all ready to go on 'oliday?' the driver asks in a thick Devonshire accent. They respond with eager nods, a polite ragged chorus of 'Yes please' and a few reserved cheers. Collectively timid. He turns back to Father and gives him another nod, this time with a big grin. Father offers him a Fisherman's Friend.

'Don't mind if I do,' he accepts, reaching into the tin. An acquired taste, there are no other takers for the extra-strong lozenges, despite Father's assurances that it would help stave off carsickness. The driver depresses his left foot on the clutch pedal, wiggles the gearstick to neutral, then turns the key in the ignition. The van starts up; he checks over his shoulder, flicks the indicator arm and pulls away.

They were off!

Father suddenly wonders if he had closed the small bathroom window, which was normally left open at all times. For the life of him he could not remember. He resists saying anything out loud, it would sound ridiculous. Instead, he assures himself that it was shut after all and puts it out of his mind.

8.
A Million Miles.

As far as father is concerned, Whitsand Bay could be a million miles from Plymouth. In fact, it is a mere seventeen. There are two possible routes into this part of Cornwall. They have the option of either crossing the river Tamar by taking the Tamar Bridge towards St Austell, or riding the vehicle ferry in Devonport to Torpoint. The driver has already made the decision to take the bridge, even though it adds a further seven miles to the journey. The risk of being delayed in a queue of cars for the summer ferry is not worth it, he reckons.

'Thought we'd take the bridge,' he announces.

'Fine by us.' Father speaks for them all.

Indeed, they are all enjoying the novelty of being driven. Father never learned to drive, due to a condition in his left eye that has left him partially blind, or at least with some reduced vision. This became a convenient excuse for avoiding the expense of purchasing and maintaining a vehicle. *What's more, they wouldn't all be able to fit in,* he reasoned with himself. It would have been an extravagant expense, one that they could not even afford, if it was just to get him to work and back. Especially when there was a perfectly adequate bus service from the housing estate into the city centre. One came along every twenty minutes.

~~~

Any family outing – a trip to the zoo, or a visit to their Aunty Betty and Uncle Hugh – was by bus, all ten of them taking up the long back seat and a few other seats as well. Father's only sister and her husband, Hugh, affectionately known as Smudge, lived on the edge of Dartmoor, in a market town called Tavistock. This journey required a change of bus at Crownhill, and the service to the moors was infrequent, so these visits needed to be regimented around the bus timetable. The time constraints often made for a shorter day than they would have wished, as Aunty Betty would spoil them with ice cream, Smudge would make them laugh, and they also got to take their Jack Russell, Peggy, out for a walk and play.

Martin suffers from motion sickness, so he would dread the journey to Tavistock. Even on bus rides to school he would often get off early and walk the rest of the way to avoid the inevitability of throwing up. Today, he has positioned himself in the second row of seats; perched dead centre, hands cupping the top of the vinyl seat in front of him. It is a rare position of privilege for the youngest. Not only to be in a private vehicle, but to have such an advantageous view, a clear sight of the road ahead and the opportunity to see how the driver actually operated the vehicle. He has an idea of how it is done but is not entirely sure about what the feet do during a gear change. He is fascinated by the coordination that is required as the driver smoothly transitions from second gear to third as they head down Millford Lane. By watching and listening he becomes able to predict when it will happen next. The engine revs to a point where the driver releases his hand from the steering wheel and reaches down for the gearstick knob; the engine noise pauses as he shifts his right foot off the right pedal, while at the same time depressing his left foot on the left pedal and also guiding the gearstick forward, across and forward again to engage the engine into a lower gear. Martin glances up at the rear-view mirror and the driver catches his eye and gives him a wink. As they slow to a stop at the junction with Budshead Road, Martin notices the driver depresses the left pedal along with the brake, then wiggles the gearstick into the middle again, like he did when they left home, before selecting first gear. Martin copies the way he looks both ways for traffic before pulling away, imagining that he is the driver.

After leaving the housing estate behind them, they need to cross the busy dual carriageway called Crownhill Road. It is a tricky turn. The junction that they are exiting is on a fairly steep hill, so the driver applies his handbrake as he waits for a decent gap in the traffic. When it comes, he finds the biting point between his left foot and right foot, releasing the handbrake to move the van forward smoothly, pausing for a second or so in the middle of the road to allow several cars to pass through before turning swiftly into the far lane as the road clears.

Impressive, thinks Martin as they pass the Blue Monkey pub.

'Blue Monkey,' says Julie, her face pressed up against the side window, giggling at the ridiculous name.

Crownhill Road leads them into St Budeaux. Bearing left here would lead them towards Devonport Dockyard and the car ferry at Torpoint, but, as announced, the van turns off right towards the highlight of the journey: crossing the Tamar Bridge, the gateway to Cornwall.

The suspension bridge has tolls, but the fee is collected at booths in the other direction, so the van is able to cruise right onto it without much of a slowdown. All the family are *oohing* and *aahing* as they stare down to take in the views of pleasure craft and fishing boats bobbing about on the river Tamar way below, the steep grassy banks leading up to the village of Saltash ahead and the formidable railway bridge adjacent. They are hopeful of seeing a train crossing this impressive span, but their schedules do not align today.

Father's gaze follows the tollbooths as they pass them. When the bridge was opened ten years earlier, they needed tollbooth operators. Although the work was considered menial, Father had considered applying. The salary was, surprisingly, significantly higher than the current wage he earned as a junior clerk with the Gas Board. He had a growing family to consider. Ultimately, though, he stuck with his current job. It just felt more secure and with better prospects (and was probably a lot less boring).

Beyond Saltash, continuing along the A38, they pass through the tiny villages of Landrake and Tideford, with steady traffic all around them. The driver prefers the quieter country lanes to the bustle of holiday traffic, so he pulls them off the main road a few miles before the main junction at Trerulefoot. It is a shortcut of sorts: shorter in distance, but slower because of the winding and narrow country lanes that they are now on. *More interesting, at least for the passengers,* he reasons, making the journey a part of the holiday. They slow down through St Germans and Crafthole, then join back up with the main road at Polbathic. They are nearly there now, the density of the traffic has fallen off as holidaymakers have peeled away to their specific destinations.

As they get closer to Whitsand Bay, they are all anticipating the first sight of the sea. The English Channel. The van makes the final turn onto the clifftop road and they strain their necks again, shifting their heads from side to side to get an unobstructed view beyond their brothers and sisters. Eventually, one of them catches a glimpse a fraction before anyone else.

'I can see the sea!' Kathy exclaims. Immediately they all see it. A dark-grey expanse marking the horizon, occasionally lost behind a dip in the road, a roadside tree or a scrubby bush. After another bend the van is now running parallel with the coast, providing a clear view for all on the right side. Even Martin is turning to take it all in. He has been so focused on the operation of the van that he does not realize that he has not felt carsick at all. Next, they are all searching for a familiar landmark, and it is Father who points it out first.

'There's the wreck!'

In the middle of the bay, about half a mile out, is the unmistakable sight of a ship's mast – a casualty of the Second World War, torpedoed by a German U-boat – rising out of the water, black against the dark grey of the sea.

～～

The driver is happy to see an available parking space opposite the cliff path. He gently guides the van off the road and brings it to a stop. Over warnings from the parents not to stray into the road, the family disembark and stretch. For the next ten minutes they unload their belongings from the back of the van, piling them up near the mouth of the cliff path on a grass clearing to one side, Mother watching out for traffic as they cross back and forth with armfuls. Aside from a single car and a pair of motorcycles the road is quiet. The driver eases out the last pieces of luggage, two large suitcases, guiding them to the ground in gentle somersaults. He confirms with Father that they have removed everything from the vehicle following a quick once-over. They shake hands and the driver says,

'See you in a fortnight.'

'Right you are,' replies Father, 'twelve o'clock, Saturday after next.'

There is no exchange of payment – an extra treat taken care of by his boss, who feels guilty for not being able to bring them all in his own car.

Left alone, now all they have to do is get everything down the cliff.

9.
Ferndale.

'Right!'

Father squashes a couple of pliable carrier bags filled with beach towels under each arm, then picks up a couple of the biggest, heaviest suitcases. The bungalow is over halfway down the appropriately named Wiggle Cliff, about a quarter of a mile along the narrow winding path. He sets off by example; the others following his lead, picking through the pile to select manageable loads. Mother oversees this process and waits with the remaining items; not that anyone would steal anything, but rather to not let it seem that these things had just been dumped here without regard. The family string out in an evenly spaced march downhill, like ants. Father has placed his first load in a clearing about fifty yards down the path, just before it bends around the corner out of sight. He is striding back purposefully to fetch another batch, tucking in each time to allow the others to pass. When Mother spots him on his way back that is her cue to gather her own share. She throws a long-handled tote over one shoulder, then picks a couple of the food bags, one of which contains the bumper-sized box of tea bags and Rich Tea biscuits. Her plan is to continue all the way down to the bungalow to open it up. After passing all the children as they trudge back up for another load, she does not meet anyone for the rest of the journey and soon finds herself at a junction with an unmarked path that descends steeply back on itself. It leads to the kitchen door at the back of the house that will be their home for the next two weeks. She locates the key under a flat stone by the drain and unlocks the door.

There is a certain mustiness about the house: partially because of the build-up of summer heat from the secured windows and door, but there is also a faint odour of gas. There is no electricity, so kerosene is the power source for the cooker and the lights. Mother goes about airing the place out by flinging all the windows wide open. Next, she returns to the kitchen, wedging the outer door ajar, both for extra light (as it is a solid door with no window), but also so the family can have direct access for the luggage drop-off. She reaches up to a high shelf to unscrew the valve at the top of the kerosene tank, which releases a flow of gas to the cooker. She pulls an oversized kettle from the open shelf and fills it for the tea they will need when they arrive. The stovetop kettle is a spare that they had brought with them a few years before and deliberately left behind, along with a similarly proportioned teapot and cosy. A box of matches is near the stove. She turns the burner knob and strikes a match to light the flame, placing the kettle on the ring. Once that is set up she uses the brief moment of solitude to take it all in: re-acquainting herself with the familiar surroundings, checking for any improvements that Mr Symons may have undertaken during the spring.

Still no fridge, she thinks to herself.

Their home back in Plymouth was small for them all, but Ferndale, the bungalow Mr Symons named for his hometown in the Rhondda Valley in Wales, was even smaller. Not that any of them minded. Being at Whitsands was the highlight of the year. An adventure. They particularly loved this little house.

Mr Symons built it mostly by himself over a couple of summers without an architect or structural engineer. It was not even inspected, nor did he submit building plans. The land was cheap but overgrown. He planned for a summer cottage, one that he would close down for the other three seasons. The site was a challenge and he made certain decisions based on access and the lack of utilities. First, he made a clearing by hacking away at the vegetation, then he levelled out the land as best he could without the aid of heavy machinery, which resulted in the house having a notable slope towards the sea. (It also creaked and shook when occupants moved about with heavy feet.) Rough framing came next – the skeleton of the house – including interior and exterior walls as well as the roof and the beginnings of the floor. After framing, and before closing up the walls with plaster, he installed rough plumbing for the kitchen and the gas lines for the interior lighting fixture locations. The exterior work was just a waterproof sheathing, no insulation required, clad in a scallop-shaped shingle vinyl siding in a fern-green colour with a black asphalt roof. To finish, the windows were installed, vinyl tiles laid down on the floors, ceilings and walls painted, interior doors hung, windowsills trimmed. The cooker appliances were delivered, and a sink installed around a basic, open-shelf kitchen. Lighting fixtures were installed, carpets laid. Furniture was carried down the cliff – bed frames and mattresses, a sofa, a dining table and chairs, a sideboard, bookshelves and dressers – then placed in position. He built a simple outbuilding, separate from the house, to accommodate a bucket toilet, digging a pit nearby to store the sewage after collection (which would be Father's unenviable job this fortnight). There is no bathroom or shower. For the next two weeks, a dip in the salty sea was going to be the best option for getting relatively clean.

～

The finished layout began with a galley kitchen, which led to a hallway with two small bedrooms either side. The kitchen was closed off with a curtain. It opened up to the living/dining area with a large picture window framing the unobstructed ocean view. The master bedroom was off to one side. Without

a fridge they relied on a cool box located in a shaded spot outside the kitchen. There was nothing technical about it: just a
small cupboard mounted at eye-level to the exterior wall with
a chicken-wire covering and a securing latch. Here they kept
their eggs, milk and butter: the perishable essentials they could
not stock up on for the full two weeks but would need to shop
for every day. The shop was a mile's walk away. There was no
electric supply to the cliff houses, so lighting was managed
with the gas lamp fixtures mounted on the walls. The gas to
the fixtures was turned on and off with a built-in valve, and
the sound of the hissing gas before the flame was applied was
something that the family always noticed, perhaps with a small
sense of danger and excitement. The best feature of the house,
they all agreed, was the veranda. A narrow balcony of sorts that
ran the length of the front of the house, overlooking Whitsand
Bay. When the tide was at its lowest you could see the breaking
waves, but mostly the view was of the sea itself, the steep slope
of the cliff and the scrubby brush obstructing any beach view.

Mother is leaning on the veranda rail now, taking it all in:
the sound of the crashing waves below and the cry of seagulls
above, the salty smell in the air, the vast ocean before her, the
feel of the sun on her face as it finally breaks through; as if it
had been waiting just for her, for this quiet moment.

~~~

Meanwhile, Father sets his latest load – a heavy crate full of
garden vegetables, with three pints of milk nestled snugly among

them – down on a welcoming bench. Hands on hips, he takes a breather, gazing out towards the glistening, bottle-green sea. Thirsty work. He reaches for one of the pints of milk, roughly presses his thumb into the silver foil cap, then proceeds to glug it down. All of it, in one satisfying draft. He wipes his lips with the back of his hand, puts the empty bottle back in the crate, picks it up with a grunt and heads off for the next gathering point; deciding not to take full advantage of the bench, but to crack on.

This laborious introduction to the fortnight is all part of the Whitsand experience for him. Something that he looks forward to; that he actually enjoys. Not to be treated as a chore to be overcome before the holiday can begin properly, but rather, an essential part of it.

10.
The Boiler.

After the cliff descent, the three youngest boys throw their bags into their room, then quickly scout out the house. Their first order of business is to head all the way down the cliff to the beach. Unpacking can wait. It does not seem right to spend time filling drawers and stowing away shoes when they have not even felt the sand between their toes yet. Amid the confusion of the mass unload going on with the rest of the family, they take advantage of the moment to disappear back up the path that they have just come down a few minutes before, which is the long way around. There is a shortcut path that leads from the front of the cottage, but they know from experience that it will be overgrown, so they do not even bother checking it. Father would clear it first thing after unpacking. It was like a ritual for him. A tradition. He preferred to do it by himself. He had actually created the path during that very first summer. Apart from being a useful exercise, at the time it was a way for him to channel the anger and sorrow he was feeling for the loss of his youngest daughter earlier that year. Now it just needs its annual maintenance. He will don his gloves, find the hedge clippers, the rake and small scythe stored under the outhouse and go about hacking away at the long grasses and prickly thistle that have encroached on the clearing, gathering up all the cuttings behind him as he goes. Once he reaches the junction with the main path, he will rake them all back up the path, collecting and stacking this for a bonfire in the side garden later that day. When Father would announce to them that the path was clear to use, they could not wait to charge down it again.

⌇

Meanwhile, the boys are racing down the cliff path as fast as they dare, the beach now tantalizingly in sight. The steepness of the descent means that the narrow path zigs and zags. Between one of these turns there are signs of a direct shortcut: a barely there, disturbed line between the established course. David, the bravest of the three, currently at the back of the group with no chance of passing, takes this opportunity by skimming down on his backside, using his feet and palms as rudders. He arrives dusty and just a little sore, but rewarded with a lead over his more conservative brothers, and the prize of first to the beach guaranteed to be his. He celebrates with arms aloft as he takes the short set of ragged steps that lead directly onto the sandy beach. Because of the overcast weather there are just a few families lying on blankets or sitting in beach chairs, mostly on the edge of the rock line. Their children are busily industrious with the sand, building dams for the incoming tide or castles with empty moats. The boys barely notice them. They know this beach intimately, and the one feature that makes it unique. They run over to inspect it first: a partially submerged ship's boiler the size of a truck, and broken parts of a hull – rusted wreckage from a ship that ran aground in fog in the early nineteen-thirties, and which has remained nestled among the rocks ever since, deeply embedded in the sand. They clamber all over it, its edges made smooth by decades of tidal sea water, now covered in barnacles.

'Seems a bit lower than before,' Peter suggests, jumping down from it, his feet sinking into the wet sand. Winter storms have indeed shifted the topography, confirmed further by their next stop on the tour: The Flat Rock. This was a massive slab that had settled horizontally, safely cantilevering beyond the rock line to offer a cool, shady spot out of the sun under its mass. It looked like a giant diving board. This would always be the first-choice spot that the family would secure for their daily base camp if it was available. The smaller rocks around it offered back support for those that wanted to read or sit upright for sandwiches. The flat surface of the rock itself was an elevated vantage point for observing the goings on of the beach, or a launchpad for the more energetic. It was high enough that the smaller boys could stand straight up underneath it. Mother would store the lunch pails and beverages in its shade.

'It's got lower too.'

Martin, the youngest, stoops slightly underneath it, neglecting to observe that he has grown three inches since his last visit.

They climb up and sit on its front edge, all in a row, feet dangling, taking in their first view of the beach this year and enjoying the sound and sight of the crashing waves. Until David, restless, gets up and walks to the back of the rock, turning and sprinting between them, hurling himself up and out, landing and rolling in the soft sand. The others gleefully follow suit, jogging to the back of the rock, climbing up and repeating their leaps, again and again in turn. Before long, the tide has become a factor. They need to time their leaps to avoid landing in the water, so they abandon their plastic sandals, making their approach along the rock a little less spirited. But it is more enjoyable as they splash into the water, holding their landings like gymnasts, their feet sinking further into the wet sand with the retreating surf. Rather than get too wet as the tide gets higher, and because fatigue is beginning to seep in, they decide to conserve their energy for the walk back up the cliff. Most families have already packed up, the beach disappearing quickly, which means that holidaymakers will shift all their belongings onto the rocks and sit it out if they wish to stay longer. The boys trudge back up the cliff, taking the path the long way around for the only time they will need to this year.

Back at Ferndale, the rest of the family are enjoying a cup of tea. Mother pulls the lid off Mrs Fryer's biscuit tin and offers the cakes around.

'What are they?' asks Kathy, peering in before committing.

'Mrs Fryer's Welsh cakes.'

'Ugh! I don't like them. They're dreadful!'

'Really?' says Father, taking a bite from one. After chewing on it for a while, with Kathy watching him for a verdict, he has to agree.

'Bit dry,' he says eventually, returning it to his plate, not to be touched again, and reaching to the teapot for a refill.

'Well,' says Mother, putting the lid back on the tin, 'it's the thought that counts.'

~~~

The boys take off their shoes before entering the cottage, turning them upside down and noticing the satisfying little stream of sand falling from each of them, as if to signify their change of circumstance from the city to the sea.

After the excitement of the journey, the unpacking, and the first visit to check out the beach, they are left in that moment where they vaguely wonder what they are going to do next, as if arriving was the thing that they were focused on. The anticipation of it all.

11.
One, Two, Three, Flash!

Everything has already been efficiently put away, aside from the three boys' holdalls, which remain in a pile where they had flung them into their room. The fourth brother has claimed his bed. Just as it is back at home there are two sets of bunk beds here. He is lying on the top one on the right side, reading the latest issue of 'Roy of the Rovers'.

The girls' room is narrower than the boys', so only has a footprint for one single bed. However, it contains a triple-decker bunk, the top level so high that there is a risk of banging your head on the ceiling if you forget where you are when waking up.

Unlike at home, Mother and Father have the main bedroom at the front of the house, which overlooks the view of the ocean. This leaves Kevin in the living/dining room, with the chore of unfolding the sofa bed last thing at night, then being harassed to get up by hungry siblings anxious to move him out of the way to access the dining table for breakfast. The table folds away when not in use; hinged sections hanging down from the side that can be raised and secured when more surface area is needed.

~~~

Mother is preparing supper with Lorraine and Julie. They decide to make something special – minced beef with onions, mashed potato and peas – rather than the beans on toast they had planned. Kevin is opening up and setting the table: laying the tablecloth and pulling the plates and cutlery from the sideboard. When the announcement is made that dinner is ready, everyone lines up in the hallway to receive a plate, cafeteria style. This family has never dished from the table; Mother prefers to serve straight from the kitchen, keeping the food as hot as possible and minimizing the use of serveware, therefore less dishes to wash up. As he turns towards the dining room with a full plate, Peter exaggerates the noticeable slope from the back of the house to front as he passes the much-amused waiting line, pulling himself along with the help of the doorways.

'Good job we're not having soup,' Kevin says to laughter.

Each of them finds their seat to match the same arrangement they follow back at home. Here it means that the three chairs with their backs to the window get boxed in when the two children sit at the hallway end. They cannot leave without making the others get up. Martin finishes his meal quickly and is keen to leave the table but realizes that is not possible quite yet without much disturbance. So, he has another idea and slides down onto the floor and snakes his way out between legs, continuing to crawl away beyond the table in the hope that he will get out of clear-up chores. No such luck, as Father allocates the three boys the job of clearing the table, washing and drying, to make up for their disappearance during the afternoon.

～～

David was fascinated by fire. He could spend hours in the garden by himself, assembling small piles of leaves and twigs, then taking out his pocket magnifying glass that he always carried with him, directing it over the pile. He would marvel at how the convex lens focused the beam at one single point, concentrating the energy that would cause these flammable objects that he had assembled to catch fire, gently blowing on it to help it along.

So, it was only natural that he would volunteer to light the gas lamps as twilight crept into the cottage each evening. Starting with the lamp nearest the picture window, he asks Julie to move out of her seat while he kneels on it. A prepared match in one hand, and the matchbox nestled in the palm of his other, he opens the supply valve. The sound of the hissing gas makes all the family pause their activities to observe. David strikes the match against the rough strip on the side of the box, the friction causing it to flame. He waits for it to die down a little, turning the match into the flame to keep it alight, then moves it towards the fabric that covers the mantle through a hole in the bottom of the glass globe, being careful not to touch the fragile mantle itself. It ignites with a satisfying *pop*, the smell of the kerosene not unpleasant and the constant hissing a comfort. He blows out the match, then adjusts the valve to regulate the amount of light in the room; not too high just yet as it is only just beginning to grow dark. He crosses the room to the other lamp on the opposite side and Julie returns to her seat.

'That's better.' She adjusts to the new ambience, locating the next question in her quiz book, which she has been reading aloud to anyone who is paying attention.

David steps up, onto the cushion of the sofa, finding a narrow space between two of his brothers, wedging his feet close together, facing the wall. He balances himself by gripping the top of Kevin's head, using the springs of the seat to propel himself gently forward, knees resting on the sofa backrest. Kevin isn't bothered. He continues reading his book. David performs the same operation as with the previous lamp, which produces the exact same gratifying *pop*. The evening has officially begun.

Julie continues:

'OK,' she projects so that all can hear. 'From which classic children's book is this the first line:

> *'Roger, aged seven, and no longer the youngest*
> *of the family, ran in wide zigzags, to and fro,*
> *across the steep field that sloped up from the*
> *lake to Holly Howe, the farm where they were*
> *staying for part of the summer holidays.'*

Kathy looks up. She cannot believe it. She has only just started reading this book, which she found on the small shelf in their bedroom, nestled among a selection of other classic titles. *Swallows and Amazons,* by Arthur Ransome. Holding the paperback aloft, she cries out:

'*Swallows and Amazons!*'

Julie immediately flips to the back of the magazine and efficiently locates the answer in the section that she has bookmarked with her right middle finger.

'Correct,' she announces, glancing suspiciously at her beaming younger sister.

'I'm reading it! *Swallows and Amazons.* I'm reading it right now. Look!'

Kathy is so happy and goes on to describe the premise of the story while Julie waits patiently to present the next question.

'It's about the adventures of these two families during the school holidays. Like us and the Lanes, I suppose. But probably a bit more exciting.'

~~~

As the evening draws on, the view from the window gradually changes to an inky blackness. Kathy has been watching it happen for a while: it is not much to look at, but she is waiting for something. It is rare to witness such pitch-dark. The cloud cover has meant that there are no stars or moon to provide any illumination tonight, and the reflection on the inside of the house causes her to press her face close to the glass, cupping the sides of her head with her hands to reduce the glare. Then she sees it. She watches it silently at first, and then gets into the rhythm, mouthing quietly:

'One, two, three, flash! One, two, three, four, five, six, seven, flash!'

The Eddystone Lighthouse sits on the horizon, about twelve miles out. The family were not aware of its significance, but it was the very first lighthouse to be built on a small group of rocks in the open sea. An important piece of architecture. Its rotating lantern has issued warnings in some form for over three hundred years. The children especially pay attention if there is a fog, the sound of its horn traveling all the way to the coast every thirty seconds.

When Kathy is sure she has the timing down, she repeats the code a little louder, so that some of the others look up. They know what is happening; the rhythmic flash identifying the unique location of the lighthouse to mariners. A couple of them join her at the window and form a chorus with the count. 'One, two, three, flash! One, two, three, four, five, six, seven, flash!' Eventually they all join in, whether they are even looking up at the flash or not. It has become another annual tradition.

On the first night, they all lay in their beds, listening to the crashing sound of the waves below and the incessant chirping of crickets. It feels like it will be too loud for them to ever fall asleep, but it soon becomes a white noise, and they will not even think about it again for the rest of the holiday.

12.
The FA Cup.

Each morning, two of the children are tasked with shopping for the perishables – milk, butter, bread – plus the daily newspaper. Basic groceries can be found at Bellamy's Cafe at the top of the cliff, a little way along from their path. All the items for purchase are displayed behind the counter at the back of the shop, rather than the usual self-serve/basket style. Mrs Bellamy seems to run the place by herself, serving customers (seated either at the picnic tables in the front garden or in the window seats at the front of the cafe) with Cornish cream teas of buttered scones, clotted cream and strawberry jam, and pots of tea, as well as serving the shoppers standing in line. If the shopping list is more complex – perhaps with the need for fresh fish or minced beef, for example – then it requires a trek inland:

along country lanes, passing through Stone Farm to the Co-op in the village of Millbrook. On this first morning, it being Sunday, the family would go together to attend the Catholic service that took place in the village hall and shop for groceries afterwards, making good use of extra hands for carrying shopping bags. Ten pasties would be secured at the local bakery, which would be their Sunday tea.

Access to the village hall was through a small, unmarked door, which felt like the tradesman's entrance. As you crossed the threshold it did not feel like you were about to step into a community space at all, nor a place of worship. It was as if the service was clandestine. The boys go along out of obligation, and perhaps tradition, their faith waning the older they become. They are greeted by a friendly elderly usher, who is dressed in a scruffy-looking three-piece suit and tie and obviously takes pride in his role. He assesses the large family group seriously, before guiding them to two empty pews at the rear of the hall, silently and reverently opening his palm as an invitation to take their seats. He waits until they have all passed him, each one getting a big grin and nod, before he heads back to the entrance. Mark has been observing him closely, captivated by his most prominent feature. He likes to give out nicknames, so he immediately connects the old man's enormous pair of ears to a relatable inanimate object. Once they are all settled into place, he nudges David seated next to him with his elbow and whispers 'The FA Cup,' while nodding in the direction of the receding gentleman, whose ears glow in the sunlight that is shining through a window above the altar. David follows his gaze but does not understand.

'FA Cup,' repeats Mark, nodding and raising his eyebrows, then mimicking lifting the iconic trophy by its oversized handles, just as the winning captain at Wembley would do. David scoffs and disguises his amusement as a throat-clearing cough. He passes on the joke with the accompanying gesture to Peter next to him, who grins widely, and who in turn leans over to Martin to share. Martin does not get it at all because by now the usher has taken his seat in the front row and is lost to view. Father shushes them. He is aware that they get bored at church, and when they are bored they can become mischievous and silly. Kevin is on the other side of Father so he is spared inclusion on the juvenile observation.

Mother and the girls are in the row in front of them, kneeling on hassocks, saying their silent prayers. The priest wanders out towards the congregation. He is not dressed for the part yet, as it is still five minutes until showtime (as Kevin refers to it). The priest smiles benignly, scanning the crowd, and his eyes settle on the row of five boys and their father in the back. Kevin notices him bend down to talk to someone nearby, evidently giving an instruction before retreating 'off-stage'. The FA Cup stands up, his back profile making Mark, David and Peter snicker. They all watch him genuflect in the aisle, then turn and come towards them with an earnest expression on his face, staring directly at them. The boys are suddenly a little worried that, somehow, the priest, through an act of God perhaps, has found out about this new nickname and that they will be punished for making fun of his gigantic ears. They squirm in their seats as the kind old man approaches. Mark lowers his head in mock prayer; David and Peter are suddenly interested in their hymn books and bury their faces in them. He reaches their row and politely raises a finger to get Father's attention, then bends down to match his eye level. Father leans forward and across Kevin in the aisle seat.

'Our altar boy hasn't shown up, would one of your sons be able to step in?' Father immediately turns towards Kevin for a response.

'Oh, I dunno.'

Kevin rubs his chin nervously, eyeing up the makeshift altar. 'It's a different set up than I'm used to.'

'You'll be fine. He'll do it,' offers Father, nudging his son to go along. Julie turns and stage whispers over her right shoulder to the boys. 'What's going on?'

'FA Cup,' Mark whispers back, as the old gentleman leads Kevin down the aisle.

'What?' Coupled with an exaggerated puzzled face.

'They need an altar boy,' Father tells them all, in a quiet enough voice. Martin starts giggling.

'FA Cup!' he whispers, which sets the others off too.

~~~

The service starts as usual, although the family are all keenly watching Kevin's performance. Things are going along without note until he is required to do something that he has done a hundred times before: carry the Bible – already opened at the required spread – to the podium for the priest to deliver the scripture reading. This set-up is different from the one he is used to. For a start, this Bible looks bigger. Much bigger. And heavier. It is off to one side of the altar, not at the back where it normally would be. Also, although the top of the lectern is angled just the same for readability, what he does not notice is that it has a recessed top, rather than the raised wooden strip along the bottom edge that he normally would rest the book against. His parish priest, Father Smith, refers to it as his pencil stopper. The priest is already in position, just a short step back from the podium; his arms bent at the elbows, palms facing inwards, ready to move forward and quote from the holy book when it arrives. Normally Kevin would come in from the left side, prop the book on the lectern, then back away with head bowed. But, because of this confined set-up, the path he would like to take is compromised; so he improvises, awkwardly reaching over the top of the lectern from the front and sliding the book into position. Without the pencil stopper it keeps sliding beyond the edge and he loses control of the heavy tome as it thuds to the floor at the feet of the priest, who merely smiles at Kevin, thinking that if anyone was dropping off before, they will certainly be paying attention now. Jaws drop in the back two rows before giving way to stifled laughter. Kevin, in the meantime, mumbles something about pencil stoppers as an apology to the priest, setting the Bible back in place with his help. He backs away, not daring to glance into the back rows of the congregation as the priest calmly flips the pages, searching for the right verse.

~~~

Outside, after the service, the children are all very amused listening to Kevin's explanation for his mishap.

'But Father Smith has a pencil stopper!' he insists once again.

'If you think it's so funny Mark Robert you can be the altar boy next Sunday,' admonishes Father, singling out the one most delighted, including his middle name for emphasis, which has the desired effect, as Mark relents from ribbing his older brother's butterfingers.

Mark's face hardens.

'That lad better show up next week,' he mutters contritely.

13.
Pop Pickers.

'Greetings Pop Pickers! How we doing? It's me again, *Fluff. Sunday at four means Pick of the Pops! Alright?'*

Alan 'Fluff' Freeman pauses for his theme song, a jazzy burst of upbeat horns and crashing cymbals, before starting up again with his signature rapid delivery, peppered with catchphrases. He fades down the music to announce the bands that have dropped out of the top twenty.

'We've lost The Mojos and Manfred Mann this week. Are we *ready for the countdown? Not 'arf!'*

Kevin adjusts the tuning knob on his portable Mitsubishi transistor radio as another blast of the disc jockey's theme builds the tension. The weekly chart rundown is essential listening and Kevin needs to concentrate. There would be too many siblings stuck inside the cottage causing distractions on this drizzly afternoon, so he is on his way up for one of his solo walks along the top of the cliff. However, the reception is spotty, the signal keeps tuning in and out. He is hoping it will improve the higher he gets. He has the hood of his anorak pulled up tight over his head, which helps keep his ultra-lightweight, collapsible headphones in place, but the sound is still tinny.

'Let's have a bash,' says Freeman. *'Onwards and upwards. New at twenty, Chairmen of the Board, they're "Working on a Building of Love".'*

Pretty soon he passes Julie, also hooded against the elements. She is gathering blackberries from the bushes for a crumble; putting most of them into a bowl, eating some.

'Where are you going?'

'What was that?'

'Where. Are. You. Going?' she asks again deliberately, aware that he has music in his ears.

'Onwards and upwards,' he says, then waves to her at close range and carries on.

〰

Kevin likes to take these cliff walks by himself; the chance for solitude is rare with such a large family. Plus, he has a lot to think about. He will be starting college next month in Southampton; moving away from home for the first time. Which, now that he thinks about it, means that his parents will probably take over his bedroom. They will finally have their own room, rather than the pull-out bed in the living room that they have been using for years.

'Down at number eighteen, it's the star-man himself, David Bowie. "Starman"...'

He has just finished a summer job, spending the last six weeks as a porter at Mount Gold Hospital in Plymouth. His job was to ferry patients to and from their wards to surgery, driving an electric vehicle similar to a milk float around the sprawling campus. Another task was to clean up the theatre post-surgery, which required a high-pressure hosepipe, buckets, scouring brushes, disinfectants, Wellington boots and a pair of heavy-duty Marigold rubber gloves. As if that thankless task was not bad enough, he was also required to collect and incinerate amputated limbs – waiting for him, wrapped in plastic, at the back of the theatre – which would have been a distressing chore for most teenagers. He had to carry a full leg last week, which was surprisingly heavy. He was unfazed by the work, which could have been traumatizing to some, and he took it all in his stride. As the oldest child in the family he felt a responsibility to set a good example to his brothers and sisters. His parents never requested it of him, he just naturally assumed this role. Kind, calm and steady.

'Think I'm gonna play some rock and roll. Up at number thir-teen, goes Gary Glitter and The Glitter Band, "Rock and Roll Part One"...'

Kevin is thinking about what to do with his earnings. He

feels cash-rich, never having actually earned a wage before. He has had his eye on a record player all summer. A two-speed Panasonic Turntable with stereo speakers. Fifty-five quid. Plus, he has a list of albums that he wants to buy. He goes over them in his mind: Deep Purple; Jethro Tull; Derek and the Dominos; Ten Years After; Savoy Brown; Elmer Gantry; Zoot Money; Yes; Emerson, Lake & Palmer; The Betterdays; The Artwoods; The Zombies . . . And he knows where he will get them, too, having bought the hit single 'All the Young Dudes' by Mott The Hoople for forty-five pence from Henry's Records when he visited Southampton in the spring. At three pounds each, he can now afford his own top-twenty albums.

'Getting serious now. At number eight, "Sylvia's Mother" by Dr Hook & the Medicine Show . . .'

The drizzle begins to strengthen into proper rain, sheeting sideways with the wind, so Kevin turns against it to head back down the cliff to Ferndale and thoughts of Sunday tea.

I'm guessing pilchards on toast, followed by blackberry crumble and custard, he thinks.

He has timed his return perfectly, as Alan Freeman runs through the countdown recap just before he will arrive back at Ferndale, only the number one song remaining to be played in the show.

'Now here's the top five Pop Pickers, and then some! How you doing gang, alright? Up to number five, it's Hot Butter, with "Popcorn". Staying at number four, Donny Osmond, "Puppy Love".'

Another pause for a few seconds of the theme song again, 'At the Sign of the Swingin' Cymbal'.

'*Up to number three, Hawkwind, "Silver Machine". Staying at number two, Terry Dactyl and the Dinosaurs with "Seaside Shuffle". Which means . . .*' he pauses for a double blast of horns that is accompanied by the incessant backing of drums, bongos and a jangling triangle. Kevin pauses too, standing at the entry to Ferndale's path.

'*For the second week . . .*' Another pause for the music, a longer clip this time (and which features a flute solo), '*. . . This week's number one song on the hit parade . . .*' The theme song ends on a series of paired trumpet blasts, then a crescendo to an abrupt silence. Impressively timed. Fluff whispers conspiringly, '*Alice Cooper. "School's Out".*'

The opening guitar riff follows dramatically, as Kevin nods along with enthusiastic approval, the appropriateness of the song title not lost on him. He stands there, listening to the number one song until it fades out, then he turns down the steep path to the cottage, pausing again to listen to Fluff's sign-off.

'*Until next Sunday at four—*' he pauses once again and fades up the music, '*Alright?*' Followed by another pause for his theme song. '*Stay Bright!*' One final musical blast, and then Fluff gives his signature farewell.

'*Ta-ta!*'

'Ta-ta!' replies Kevin, before removing his headphones and clicking off the radio, then kicking off his wet shoes outside the kitchen door.

14.
A Band of Rain.

On a normal Monday morning, Father would arrive at the office at around eight thirty, preparing the stations for each cashier, opening the safe and allocating one hundred pounds of change in various denominations of notes and coins, double-checking the amounts as he loads up the tills. Next out of the safe would be the ledgers, to be placed in position on the desks in front of each customer window. From a cupboard behind the counter, he would retrieve the ink stamps and pads, rotating the number and day to reflect today's date, then placing them at the head of each ledger. He would pull up the blinds on each customer window, polishing the glass with Windex and a soft cloth. Then he would put the kettle on. The rest of the staff start arriving around ten minutes before nine. Aside from being a place where the public go to pay their gas bills, it is also a show-room for appliances: cookers, fridges and freezers. A couple of salesmen work the floor, including Bill Symons. Father's normal day would be spent dealing pleasantly with the public. Some of the customers he had known for years, to whom he would chat beyond just exchanging pleasantries. He would often listen to their opinions or stories, which he would then relate to the family at dinner time.

'This old feller came in today. He's eighty-seven. Smokes a pack a day. Tells me he's as fit as a fiddle! He had a bit of a wheezy laugh though. His mother lived until she was hundred and four. Maybe it's in his genes . . .'

'Ah, you wouldn't want to be that old,' says Mother, not a question but a statement.

'Why would it be in his jeans?' asks the youngest.

'G.E.N.E.S.,' says Julie, literally spelling it out for him. The aspiring nurse then tries to explain what genes are. 'They're the things inside us that figure out what we look like, and lots of other stuff too.'

'What else?'

'Well, like how you've got dark hair and David's is fair. That sort of thing.'

'Anyway,' continues Father, 'he says to me that he worked at the dockyard for forty years, as a welder. Then he says that this one ship they worked on was haunted.'

This gets everyone's attention.

'A ghost appeared every day on the bridge, at five o'clock on the dot.'

Father pauses.

'Who was it?' asks Lorraine, "was it the captain?'

'Maybe the captain fell overboard and his ghost came back,' suggests Mark.

Father takes a mouthful of potato, waiting for the right question.

'Did anyone see it?' asks Peter.

'That's what I asked him. He said they all knocked off at half-past four, so no-one ever did.'

There is a silence while they all try to figure out what they were just told. Father starts to smile.

'He had us there for a while, didn't he?'

~~~

He liked people. It was the reason that he stayed in the job, even turning down the chance to join the sales team, which would have meant a pay rise and the chance of commissions on sales. But he saw how they worked from his seat behind the glass – long spells of boredom, pushing customers into considering the more expensive items beyond their means, persuading them that it would be worth the price. That was not for him.

~~~

This Monday morning there is no alarm clock, but he is up early anyway, eager to start the day. No need to wake the children. He still has the same breakfast of toast and tea, still listens to the news on Radio Four. But he is not standing over the sink in the kitchen. Today he is outside on the veranda, his mug of tea resting on the rail, the radio at his feet on the deck. The view is spectacular. The coastal bluff of Rame Head frames the left side, a conical hill with an intact shell of a fourteenth-century chapel at its highest point; to the right the dots of houses that form the fishing village of Looe far away – the two headlands creating Whitsand Bay. The weather is currently overcast and the forecast he hears on the radio, ominously predicting a band of rain, plus the dark gathering clouds overhead, confirms it. This will disappoint most holidaymakers, but not Father. If it is going to rain, he will get his Wellingtons and his wet-weather gear then go for a long walk along the cliff. He eyes the chapel as his destination point, imagining just how windy it might get out there, relishing the prospect.

Normally, people need a few days of adjustment to get into the holiday frame of mind, but with Father, perhaps because his job is so basic, he does not go through this adjustment period. Once he leaves the office, all thoughts of it are left behind. Rain or shine, he will make the most of the next two weeks.

～～～

The others spend most of the day stuck indoors: cursing their luck, checking the skies for a break in the weather, playing board games and reading. Peter has his dice with him and a stack of used dot-matrix computer paper that his father had brought home from work for him, the blank reverse sides perfect for his recording purposes. He makes up his own entertainment, using the dice to create football scores for his own personal FA Cup competition. For each tie he will roll the pair of dice nine times, which will equate to ten minutes of the ninety-minute game per roll. A single six means a goal for the home team, a double six is a score for the away team. Before getting to the actual games he needs to write down the names of all the teams on pieces of paper and pull them out of a hat to set the ties for the third round. He must then develop a handicap system so that it is harder for lower-level teams to beat the more distinguished clubs, factoring in a more complex home-venue advantage, etc. All of which needs to be chronicled. He is going to be busy today.

Gin Rummy is the default family card game, introduced to them by their Irish grandmother on their mother's side, as well as the source from which most of the family humour can be traced. Mother repeats all her mother's phrases and sayings, passing them on to the children. Her presence is always felt through their language.

Mother, Lorraine, Mark and David make up a foursome.

Mother wins the first hand.

'Ah, you mosey. You shouldn't have done that.'

She picks up Mark's discarded four of clubs and shuffles it into place in her own hand.

'There, there and there,' she announces, laying down three kings; a run of the four, five and six of clubs; then tagging her final card, the ten of hearts, to David's jack, queen and king of the same suit. 'Count up your dead, Bob's Your Uncle!' she concludes, brimming with delight.

'Mosey? Count up your dead? Bob's Your Uncle? Where does all that come from?' asks David as he tallies up the scores.

'Your granny. My mum.'

'What does it even mean?'

'Well, mosey is an idiot. No offence Mark.'

Mark shrugs.

'Count up your dead is from the plague I suppose, and Bob's Your Uncle is . . . I don't know actually, it just means I win!'

She raises her cocoa to toast her mother with another classic from the archives.

'Here's to you, as good as you are,

And here's to me, as bad as I am;

As bad as I am, as good as you are,

I'm as good as you are as bad as I am.'

～

Father takes the same path that he followed last year, and the year before that. It leads him steeply upwards and soon he can look back across the bay. He walks on the springy turf towards the point. Aside from some sheep nibbling on the grass nearby, he is quite alone. Despite the leaden sky and a steady drizzling rain, he rests on a moss-covered rock for a while, enjoying this moment of peace and solitude before he turns back.

15.
The Whistle.

For the next two days the weather remains remorselessly
wet. It varies from torrential downpours to a steady drizzle, but
the rain never lets up: for the most part keeping the children
stuck indoors, yet always with one eye looking out for a break
in the grey sky. David in particular has fidgeted backwards and
forwards for an hour or so, to and from the window, willing the
rain to stop, cursing the cruel drizzle. He settles down again,
absorbed in his book for a few chapters. Suddenly he looks up and
listens, and the absence of dripping water strengthens his hopes.

'I think it's actually stopped,' he announces. It had not, but
the light mist felt like it was not enough to keep some of them
inside any longer.

The high tide had just turned, so, with a bit of time to spare before lunch, the three youngest boys and Julie decide to head down to the beach, to climb the rocks and play in the pools that have formed there.

Peter leads the way down the path, and is immediately rewarded with a faceful of cobweb. Not the actual web, but the single strand of thick silk that the spider has released first, its anchor thread, attached to a branch. There are lots of cobwebs all the way down both sides of the path, made visible by the misty rain settling on them and making them glisten. Peter rubs it off his face, an irritation more than anything, then continues with his hands raised up in front of him until they join up with the wider main path to the beach. David has brought with him a short length of fishing line with a hook attached at one end. Once on the beach, and on their way over to the pools, he scrapes a couple of mussels from a group that were attached to a large rock and puts them in his pocket. They arrive at their favourite spot. It is probably the biggest rock pool – at around ten-feet-long by four-feet-wide, it looks fairly deep in parts. Seaweed covers its sides and floor, making it dark and murky. The other rocks around it are steep, so they need to be careful as they descend closer to the edge. There are smaller fish skitting around near the surface, but David is going for bigger game. Once he is in position, he splits opens one of the oval-shaped shells down the middle to reveal the soft orange fleshy body of the mussel inside. He scoops it out with one of the empty halves and attaches the meat to the hook, then dangles the line over the pool: letting it slip through his fingers, lower and lower until he has it where he wants it, tempting the larger fish that are hiding in the dark nooks and crevices. It only takes a few moments before he feels a pull on the wire, so he yanks it up quickly, standing up from his crouched position for leverage. Wriggling on the hook is a rock goby, about four inches long. It has two dorsal fins, one with a yellow tinge on top. Its eyes are bulging. Julie studies it closely as it flaps about on a flat rock.

'It's ugly.'

'What now?' asks Martin.

'I'll take the hook out and throw it back,' says David. Which is easier said than done. He is nervous about handling the struggling fish; its scaly skin is rough to the touch; he is afraid that it might try to bite his fingers as he tries to gently coax the hook from out of the side of its mouth, trying to pull it out the same way that it went in. But the barb that projects backwards from the hook is making it difficult. He actually feels like he is making the wound worse. Julie is squirming watching the protracted operation. Suddenly it becomes free and David drops the goby immediately back into the pool. They watch it disappear into the depths.

'Will it be okay?' asks Martin.

'Yeah.'

Peter is not so sure.

'You ripped its mouth apart, I don't think I'd be okay.'

Rather than join them on the beach, Lorraine has spent the late morning taking advantage of the quiet time and the break in the weather to get a start on her A level summer project. As part of her botany studies she must find and identify one hundred different samples of plant life from a single locale. She had bought a suitably large and weighty scrapbook in Plymouth the week before, something that she planned to treasure for the rest of her life. It has an attached elastic band to keep all her samples together, with over a hundred pages of parchment paper and a heavy cover, ideal for pressing. For now she leaves it on the dresser in the bedroom, ready for the first batch to be pressed into it on her return. Armed with her beach tote bag over her shoulder and a pair of kitchen scissors she makes her way up from the house to start collecting. Even before stepping onto the main cliff path she has already gathered five different varieties.

Maybe this won't be so difficult after all, she thinks, having initially being daunted by the prospect, although the real challenge will be in identifying each one. She recognizes just one of them so far: foxglove.

~~~

Mother is in the kitchen preparing sandwiches for their midday meal as Lorraine passes through towards the bedroom and her scrapbook, keen to press her collected cuttings.

'Oh Lorraine,' says Mother over her shoulder as she senses Lorraine behind her, 'will you fetch your brothers and Julie from the beach? Dinner's almost ready, I don't think we'll be going down today with this weather.'

Lorraine is torn between her mother's request and her desire to complete her project for the day.

'Can't someone else do it, Mum. I have to press these plants right away.'

'I asked you. Come on Lorraine, it's almost ready and it'll take you a while to go down and get them, so off you go.'

She sets her bag down just inside the bedroom door, noticing Kathy lying on the bed, reading as usual.

Lorraine did not have the typical traits normally expected of the second child. The parental joy of the secondborn can often be tempered compared to the first. There is less fuss, and more practicality, which can often result in a feeling of being neglected. Especially when a third child comes along so quickly. Then a fourth. And so on. But Lorraine has always felt the responsibility of a firstborn. Perhaps because she has two younger sisters who look up to her. She is reliable and conscientious. So, despite feeling a little aggrieved, she goes back outside through the kitchen.

'They're probably on the rocks,' offers Mother without turning around.

Lorraine is about to open the garden gate to start down the path, then decides to look out over the fence before setting off. She spots them in the distance, or rather, she picks out Peter's distinctive white pullover. They are way over on the rocky side of the bay, as Mother had guessed.

'I wonder,' she says to herself, deciding to try something first.

~~

Their expedition is interrupted by the unmistakable sound of a loud, long, shrill whistle. They all look up the cliff to see their oldest sister, Lorraine – only her head and shoulders visible in front of Ferndale – waving her arms above her head, beckoning them back for dinner. They wave back and start climbing away from the pool towards the beach and the cliff path.

'How does she do that?' asks Martin.

Julie explains, 'You get these two fingers, put them under your tongue like this, then roll your tongue back and just blow.'

Martin gives it a go. Nothing happens. He keeps trying without success. They each try; David not for long, because his fingers taste of mussels. As they start climbing the cliff path, Peter makes it work briefly, but he cannot repeat it. David has switched to creating another sound. He clasps his hands together, keeping both thumbs upright and pressed against each other, he bends the tops of his thumbs over a little, presses his lips against the top joint in his thumbs then blows through and down into his hands. The sound is quite satisfying. It could be the hoot of an owl or the whistle of a distant train. Peter follows suit, better at this than the whistle. Martin finally gives up, deciding to ask Lorraine for better instruction when he gets up to the cottage.

~~~

'Was that you?' asks Mother, handing Kathy a platter of corned beef sandwiches to take through to the dining room, as Lorraine slips back through the kitchen.

'They're on their way.'

Her initiative has bought her about ten or fifteen minutes to press the plants into the book.

Perfect.

She pulls them out of her bag carefully, one by one, examining each then clipping their stalks to fit within the book. She gently allocates a spread for each, starting from the rear of the book, so that the weight will be greater on them for pressing and drying. She has collected twenty species in a short amount of time and distance: cow parsley, burdock, agrimony, foxglove, two types of bindweed, knapweed, thistle, vetch, meadow grass, sea kale, bedstraw, cowslip, wild mignonette, sea campion, butcher's broom, lizard clover, brookweed and alexanders. Not that she knows their names yet – she will do her best by referencing *Botanicum*, the illustrated textbook that was assigned to her class. If the weather stays like this, she will at least be able to keep herself occupied. She hears her siblings clattering into the kitchen from the beach, the whole house shuddering with their heavy footfalls. She closes over the cover of the book and secures it with the elastic band, surprised and contented with how well that session went.

Only another eighty to go, she thinks. Daunted once again.

16.
Radio Four.

Another dull weather day has kept most holidaymakers away from the beach, which the children are using as their own private playground. Kathy and Lorraine are attempting to play badminton, but the breeze is spoiling their efforts. Julie is practising her hula hoop technique. Peter, David and Martin are throwing pebbles at tin cans that they have lined up on the ridge of a tall rock, making use of the detritus left behind by the careless day trippers. Kevin and Mark are skimming flat stones, counting the number of bounces aloud. The tide is quickly upon them today, so some return up the cliff to the chalet. Mark, David, Kathy and Peter have decided to stay down longer and watch the waves, climbing up onto the flat rock, kicking off their sandals and dangling their feet over the edge. The wind has picked up significantly, increasing the size of the waves, which are big and loud today. There is a sense among them that a storm is brewing. They are all aware of the seventh wave phenomenon: that waves come in groups of fourteen, that they increase in size until the middle one, then decrease after that, before building again.

'Here it comes,' announces David, spotting the next big wave. It crashes impressively against the rocks, the surf splashing up on them a little as it laps below. They are mesmerized as they continue to follow the distant swells, always spotting and calling out the seventh before it breaks.

At one point, Mark gazes further out to sea than the others, his eye drawn to an even larger swell than normal. He keeps watching it until it is definitely the next seventh wave.

'Oh, look at this one!' Kathy is suddenly aware of its presence too. A couple of them stand up, a little concerned with their vulnerable position; only Mark remains seated as the others start backing up slowly. It crashes right at the base of the flat rock, then washes up and over Mark, its surf streaming across the rock surface. Their sandals are flung about every which way, knocking pairs of them over the edge. Among screams and squeals of laughter they chase after their shoes before the tidal pull can carry them away. All are saved, apart from Mark's. He cannot see them anywhere and is soon resigned to the fact that the ocean has taken them, which makes his walk back up the cliff path a ginger one.

~~

Rain has been hammering hard against the window all evening. It does not matter to them if it rains at night. In fact, they are all enjoying the soothing sound.

A flash of lightning gets their attention.

'Whoa!' exclaims Mark, looking up from his book. Kevin immediately starts a count.

'Thousand and one. Thousand and two. Thousand and three. Thousand and four. Thou—'

A rumble of thunder interrupts him.

'Under a mile away,' he says with confidence. 'Did you know, you see the lightning immediately, but the sound of the thunder takes about five seconds to travel.'

After the next flash, Julie takes up the count, but does not get very far.

'Thousand and—'

A loud crack of thunder fills the room.

'That must be right overhead!' David is in awe of nature.

'Janey Mac!' exclaims Mother. No one knows who Janey Mac is, but they are familiar with hearing her name in this context.

The storm passes slowly, and they all settle back into their quiet pastimes.

~~~

'And now the Shipping Forecast issued by the Met Office on behalf of the Maritime and Coastguard Agency,' says the deep male voice over the radio later that evening. *'Viking; southwesterly five to seven; occasionally gale eight; rain or showers; moderate or good, occasionally poor.'*

Cryptic and mesmerizing, what follows is ten minutes of what most listeners consider to be a form of poetry, a soothing late-night babble of words and numbers. But to the fishermen dotted about these regions around the British Isles it is an important service, informing them of the expected weather and sea conditions overnight.

Father's portable radio is set on the dining table, tucked under the window frame, having brought it in from the bedroom to listen to the ten o'clock news. He was about to turn it off before the Met Office announcement made him pause. The older members of the family that have stayed up until after ten are enjoying night-time mugs of hot drinking chocolate. They all half-listen contentedly, while carrying on with their library books and magazines.

'Cromarty; easterly four or five, backing northerly or north-easterly five or six; slight or moderate, becoming moderate, occasionally rough later; rain at first; moderate becoming good.'

Normally, at home, they would not be listening to the radio in the evening. They would have spent their time watching the black-and-white television. On a Thursday evening, BBC One all night: *Tomorrow's World*, then *Top of The Pops* and *Mastermind*, with some staying up for *Monty Python* following the *Nine O'Clock News*.

'Dogger; easterly four or five; backing northerly or north-easterly five or six; slight or moderate, becoming moderate, occasionally rough later; rain at first; moderate becoming good.'

Apart from Father. He liked to do the washing-up after dinner and tune in to the jazz station on the same portable radio. Big-band orchestras were his favourite. Glenn Miller. Duke Ellington. Tommy Dorsey. Artie Shaw. He would make sure to close over the doors to the front room and the dining room for a double buffer, and then turn the volume way up. But on occasion the song on the radio was irresistible, too good for him to enjoy by himself. He had to dance.

Well before the distinctive opening eight bars of 'In the Mood' have transitioned into the main phase of the tune, Father bursts through the front-room door, his eyes fixed on Mother, the triumphant mix of saxophones, clarinets, trumpets and trombones joining him in the room, drowning out the television.

It is their tune.

'Uh-oh!' Peter quickly gets to his feet. They all know what to do. In order to accommodate this too-rare display of unconstrained joy, the room is hastily cleared of any obstructions, the volume on the television is turned down. The sofa gets pushed to the back wall. The two armchairs also make way, slid to each side to create an impromptu dance floor. In the meantime, Mother is pulled to her feet by Father and they begin to swing. The children pack onto the seats with their feet tucked up out of the way, looking on in awe.

Their well-practised routine, developed on the dance floors during the big-band era of their courting days, involves a choreographed sequence of synchronized spinning and swinging, pushing away and coming together, dipping and rising. As is the style, Father leads, and every time he spins Mother around the children whoop with delight. Mark is watching their feet, impressed with their coordinated, rhythmic, creative footwork.

It is all over too soon. Father bows to Mother. She curtseys, a little breathless. The children applaud and cheer wildly. Father returns to the kitchen and the furniture is re-arranged.

~~~

'Fisher; northeast four; increasing five or six, occasionally seven later; slight or moderate, becoming moderate; fair; good.'

They do not miss having a television when at Ferndale. It is different here. They each have something to keep them occupied: knitting, jigsaw puzzles, comics, novels, card tricks, marbles and dice.

'German Bight; east or northeast four or five, increasing six; slight or moderate, becoming moderate; occasional rain or thundery showers; good, becoming moderate or poor later. Plymouth...'

At the mention of Plymouth, they all pause what they are doing to listen more intently, as if they will be able to decipher the report and so adjust their plans for the next six hours accordingly. In fact, this forecast is actually much different from all of the others that preceded.

'Gale warning; northeasterly gale force eight expected later; southwesterly four or five, becoming cyclonic five to seven, occasionally gale eight later; slight or moderate, becoming moderate or rough; rain or thundery showers; good, occasionally poor.'

Raised eyebrows and concerned expressions fill the room.

'Cyclonic?' questions Kevin.

They do not follow the rest of the shipping forecast, talking over the wind, sea state, weather and visibility conditions for Humber, Thames, Dover, Wight, Portland, Biscay, Trafalgar, Fitzroy, Sole, Lundy, Fastnet, Irish Sea, Shannon, Rockall, Malin, Hebrides, Bailey, Fair Isle and Faeroes. They have had nothing but dreary days so far this week: running down to the beach between showers to play a quick game of cricket, kick a football, check out the rock pools at low tide, skim flat stones, or just going for a walk along the shore. So, the prospect of it getting worse, 'cyclonic five to seven', has them all a little frustrated.

'When is it going to be sunny?' one of them asks.

Even Father is ready for a day at the beach. He has enjoyed getting lashed by the wind and rain on his coastal walks so far, but almost a week in already and he has not even been able to lay down on a towel in the sand and take a nap. Yet he remains optimistic.

'All this rain will make you appreciate the sun more. It'll clear up. You wait and see, by afternoon it will have all blown away, blue sky, sunshine, lovely!'

He switches off the radio; the end of the report has signaled the time for bed. Some roll their eyes. Others shake their heads. A deflated bunch start preparing for bed.

But he was right.

17.
Blue Sky.

'There you are look,' announces Father, pointing out of the window with a quartered salmon paste sandwich, 'bit of blue sky. Told you.'

Indeed, a tiny strip of blue sky was breaking up the heavy clouds. It had begun to clear up during their midday meal of sandwiches and Ribena. Or, at least, it had stopped raining. Now there was cause for optimism for an afternoon on the beach. Clean-up was tackled with urgency by all of them, although Kathy was excused to go and meet her friends arriving on the bus from Torpoint for the day. However, the washing-up would have to wait for the time being. By the time the rest of the family are trooping down the cliff path the sky is predominantly blue. The sun is finally shining down on them, alternately warm on the backs of their necks, then making them squint as they turn to face it on the zigzag path. The afternoon was going to be a real scorcher! The tide was way out, possibly just about to turn, which made for perfect cricket conditions. This would be the first proper game of the holiday.

After the family claim their spot by the flat rock, four of the five boys dash out to set up the wicket. Kevin, unlike his four younger brothers, is not very sporty, but he is still keen to be part of the game, so he strolls out after them.

They play catch to begin with, just to loosen up. After a few rounds of gentle, accurate throws, one of them would hurl a skyer, then another would vary the delivery with a hard and low bounce. Good practise for fielding. By that time, they know they are about ready to set up for a proper game. They find a good spot, then set the stumps into the soft sand. Martin balances the bails on top and draws out the crease. He lays the bat down flat, following its length with a finger poked into the sand, then moves it along so that the top of the blade aligns with his mark. He measures again, just the handle length this time, then draws a line by scraping the corner of the bat parallel with the stumps. Mark marches out twenty-two steps, being careful not to step on the approach to the wicket, then drags a heel to mark the bowling line. They will need to move the wicket every couple of overs or so, the sand scuffing up too easily to allow a true bounce of the tennis ball.

They have only just begun to loosen up, getting a feel for line and length. Peter is throwing soft spinners round the wicket down the track; David returning with a defensive push towards Martin, the off-side fielder. Kevin asks if he can have a bowl, so Peter tosses him the ball. Rather than take a conventional run-up, Kevin stands on the bowling line and stares down the pitch, fixing his eyes on the batsman, cradling the ball with both hands in front of his chest, elbows tucked in. He relaxes himself with a deep breath, then pivots his weight to his back foot as he lifts his right arm above his head. He slowly windmills his arm a couple of times, still balancing on his back foot, then he speeds up the arm rotation until his arm is a blur, before shifting his weight to his front foot and releasing the ball high and wide. The boys all collapse with laughter. Kevin decides to leave the game on a high note and heads back to join the rest of the family by the rocks.

David retrieves the ball and, as he picks it up, he notices a movement on the cliff path.

'Here come the Lanes!' he announces excitedly.

They all look back up to spot a ragged group racing down the crooked path, spread out by youth and their level of eagerness to reach the beach. The Lanes. Another large family that closely resembles their own: five boys and five girls, similar in age. Their parents are schoolteachers in Kent, which means they are able to spend at least six weeks of their summer at Whitsands.

They own their own cottage, much higher up on the cliff. David assumes that they probably spotted the same patch of blue sky that they had – it just took them longer to reach the beach.

'Now we can have a proper game.'

At last, it feels like the holiday is properly underway.

Four of the Lane boys run directly out to the game. They are all happy to reunite with their summer pals, but, as with all boys at that age, their greeting is brief and at a short distance away from each other; quick waves and short exchanges. Apart from Simon, the most exuberant of them. He is babbling away, trying to catch up in one paragraph.

'Did you lot just get here? We've been here two weeks already, which means we've still got four more weeks to go. The weather's been rubbish. You only stay for a fortnight don't you? Why don't you stay longer? Chris got all his O levels. Damian got measles at Christmas. I passed my eleven-plus so I'm going to grammar school in September. Mum and Dad got me a new watch as a present, look! It's waterproof so I can wear it when I go swimming ...'

Everyone takes the opportunity to drift away as he steps closer and presents his wrist towards David, who feels a little bit trapped by this suddenly intense one-sided conversation, reminded of how irritating Simon can be.

'Wow, that's great, shall we play cricket?'

'Oh,' says Simon, cut down before he can list all the other features of his new Timex, 'yeah, alright. I suppose so.'

They are about to get down to the business of picking sides – they never pit family against family, the age make up and skill level would have been a distinct disadvantage to the Lane boys;

plus, they were about to be an odd number.

'Here comes Fred!'

Fred Davis. A likeable and confident fourteen-year-old from Yorkshire, home of cricket. He is another summer regular, spending a fortnight with his parents every year; not always coinciding with the family's schedule, but they usually overlap. He is sauntering down the cliff path with his own bat resting on his shoulder. When he sees that he has been spotted he stops to face the beach and gives a big victory wave, arms aloft, bat held high, as if he is acknowledging the adoring crowd at Headingley after yet another century.

'Hiya,' he says to them all as he reaches the group, a big easy grin covering his face. 'Whose side am I on?'

Four against five. The two youngest on the same team. Everyone fields. One batsman at a time. Six-ball overs. Everyone bowls. The rocks and the sea are the boundary. The bowler sets the field: wicketkeeper, two on, two off; one of them silly, the other deep. A third man.

The next couple of hours are glorious. Not just because of the long-anticipated cricket game, but the two families are set up next to each other and are catching up with all their news; parents sat on fold-out chairs, the girls mingling on beach towels, creating one big happy group. Kathy is with her school friends and Mary Lane, who are engaging the younger Lane children by idly helping them build sandcastles as they sit on towels and chat excitedly to each other.

It feels like summer is here at last.

18.
Wednesday-itis.

'And it's Snow, coming in from the Vauxhall End. He's up
to the wicket and bowls, outside the off stump, Engineer lets it
go through, taken by Knott. No run. Score remains two hundred
and twenty-two for six.'

The commentator pauses a beat as his attention is diverted
away from the action, or lack of it.

'Hmm. Looks like a few rather ominous dark clouds are gath-
ering on the horizon. I'll keep an eye on those.'

India are playing England in the third test at The Oval. Father
is finally getting his nap on the beach: the cricket commentary
on his bright-red portable radio lulling him, along with the
rhythm of the breaking waves, the squawk of seagulls and the
chatter of holidaymakers. He is happily drifting off, lying flat

on his back on a blanket in the sand; a towel balled up as a pillow under his head, a newspaper over his face and one knee raised.

'Snow again to Engineer. He bowls, played defensively on the leg side, fielded by D'Oliveira, no run. Snow signals to Illingworth that he wants another slip. The wind's getting up a bit now, tugging at the flag, going straight down the ground. John Snow is having to bowl into that.'

Mother is with him, along with the girls. They have packed a lunch of corned beef and pickle sandwiches, half a dozen hard-boiled eggs, individual packets of Smith's salt and vinegar crisps, a flask of milky tea and a few bottles of diluted orange juice, all zipped up in Father's work holdall placed under a shady rock.

Meanwhile, the other cricket match on the beach is abandoned when the on-side fielders are up to their ankles in surf. There is no more room for a fresh wicket, so the game is declared a draw. Stumps are pulled up and they dump the equipment near the two family groups. Some peel off their T-shirts and throw them on the pile; others are already shirtless as they charge back towards the sea for a cooling-down splash-about and swim before lunch, encouraging everyone to join them. Fred charges in first, with a high-knee-action sprint to avoid the low breaking waves. He gets as far as he can, before he is tripped up by the current, twisting and throwing himself into the water with a comical backflip. The others follow, in similar though less exuberant fashion. The Atlantic Ocean is cold, so some only get as far as their knees: pausing, then cautiously advancing

– arms raised with elbows pointing outwards, allowing the breaking waves to help them acclimatize – before marching in further and deeper. A couple of the girls have decided to join in the fun, confidently striding forward, undeterred by the frigid temperature, until they are able to meet a breaking wave by diving into it and emerging on the other side, smoothing their long hair out of their wet faces. Kevin is cautious too, having not been overheated by the exertion of games. He walks to the edge and takes a sharp intake of breath as the coldness laps over his ankles. He allows himself a few moments to get used to it before venturing further out, up to his calves, then his knees, with deep, regular breaths to combat the change in temperature. Beyond the breaking waves, the sea is up to his hips now, and he splashes himself on his arms and chest. Finally, he turns and falls backwards, puffing out his cheeks and pushing off with one foot. Not a particularly good swimmer, he prefers to float. Occasionally he will propel himself around by kicking his feet and flapping his arms about his sides, but mostly he lets the rise and fall of the tide move him about.

Although today he decides to try a ridiculous one-armed backstroke, which has him circling the group.

The youngest sits cross-legged at the bottom of a recently vacated beach blanket, picking up handfuls of sand and letting it run through his fingers, taking in the scene of frolicking siblings and friends. He does not trust the waves or the current. The sea frightens him. He could go in and play by the water's edge, but something is holding him back. Maybe they will all notice him standing there and force him to join them and go deeper. When he does not, maybe they will even try picking him up and carrying him out of his depth and dumping him there, to see if he will float. His brothers are not mean, they would not do that to him, but you never know with the others around. Best to play it safe. He cannot swim. Or at least, that is what he tells himself.

~~~

Martin did not take well to the swimming lessons with his school class, unlike his brothers and sisters before him. Most of the boys and girls of his year could already swim and were confidently enjoying themselves in the pool. Some were going for their twenty-five yard certificates, or even life-saving qualifications if they were deemed capable and willing. He is left with five other classmates who have confessed that they cannot swim either. The instructors make matters worse. They do not have any patience with his anxiety. While the others begin to pick up on the required techniques, he only manages to complete a few doggy-paddles while wearing armbands in the shallow end. He actually quite enjoys this minor accomplishment, so they assume he is ready to try without them. Which he is not. Despite their encouragement from the side, he cannot bring himself to launch into the water without any support. He struggles to find the confidence to attempt even a stroke. Their solution is to float him out towards the deep end of the pool by having him hold onto a long pole, which the instructor leads him by as she walks along the edge, reassuring him that he will be okay. She then tells him to let go of the pole and just start swimming. He does not let go. So, she eventually drops her end of the pole and he goes under. He scrambles to the edge by thrashing and panicking. The instructor is more worried about her pole than the boy crying and holding on to the side for dear life, out of his depth. He pulls himself along the edge all the way back to the shallow end and climbs up the steps out of the pool. Traumatized. After that session he would suddenly become sick on Wednesdays, feigning illness to avoid having to return to the pool. But it could not last. His parents were soon aware that Wednesday-itis was best confronted than avoided. He returned to the pool a few weeks later. It was the last class of the term and he soon was embarrassed to realize that he was now the only child in his class that could not swim. This got him special attention from the instructors. He was the final obstacle before a completely successful series of lessons. So, this time two of them walked him up the side of the pool to the deep end. Instead of the long pole they produced a harness attached to a rope. This time he was assured that they would not let go, so they fitted it around his chest and he climbed reluctantly down the steps into the pool. He was pulled across the width as he practised the breaststroke that they had shown him, kicking his legs rather than the frogs' legs style they would have preferred, but they let that go as he reached the other side without incident.

'Let's go back the other way. Ready? And go . . .'

Off he went: quick strokes, head held high, quick breaths, frantic kicking, focused on the other side of the pool. The instructor was still holding on to the rope, but he now noticed out of the corner of his eye that she had let it go slack. She was holding it with a limp wrist and smiling at him as she kept pace. He did not quite understand. As he reached and grabbed the side of the pool she told him, 'That was all you, I didn't pull you along at all. You were swimming!' She dropped the rope to the ground.

He could not believe it.

'Go on swim back to the other side, you can do it now!'

He looked across the pool. He was out of his depth. What if he did not make it? The instructor could see the fear return to his face.

'Tell you what,' she said, moving to the end of the pool rather than behind him at the side, and crouching down, picking up the rope again and reaching out towards him with her other hand, 'just push off the wall and kick over to me, two strokes and you're there.'

That did not seem too difficult. He calculated that he could just about make that distance with the momentum of the push off. She had the rope too if he started to drown. So, after a few deep breaths, he did as she said and pushed off. Remarkably, he performed a stroke that propelled him buoyantly forward, then another. Feeling inspired, instead of reaching for the pool edge he turned and kept going towards the other side.

'Fantastic!' called his instructor, 'keep going, keep going!'

When he reached the side, he paused for just a second then turned and pushed off again, actually swimming back the other way.

'That's it! Well done! You'll get your twelve-yard certificate for this!'

He was so happy! He reached the side safely, found the steps and climbed out of the pool so that they could take the harness off him, then they told him to join the others in the shallow end and practise. He was so proud of himself. His classmates were too busy having fun to notice him join them. He had every intention of practising, but it was busy at this end; kids were splashing about, jumping around, going under and popping back up. He did not have a clear lane to the other side. So he just stood there, dipping his shoulders under now and again, but not attempting another stroke. He started to think it was just a fluke, maybe they did pull him after all. He stayed in limbo like this until the whistle rang out to signal the end of class. His family all told him how much more he was going to enjoy his holidays at Whitsands now.

Every now and again he would pull out his twelve-yard swimming certificate from the little cubby by his bedside, just to convince himself that he had actually done it. It was not on display, just nestled in among his books and the one other recognized accomplishment from that year: first place in the wheelbarrow race at the school sports day. He had confidence in that achievement. He and his friend, Mike Richards, had practised for days before. It was a full-pelt charge; his friend was the driver while he was the wheelbarrow, held by his ankles, desperately trying to keep up with rapid hand slaps on the grass: all he could do to prevent a painful face plant. Fear propelled him. They won by a mile.

But he still had not conquered the fear of the water, despite his success in the pool.

19.
Bullocks.

On the second Sunday of their holiday they return to Millbrook village for morning Mass. The walk takes them along a public footpath that passes through Hillside Farm. The strong smell of manure precedes it. The farm dog, a Border Collie, barks a warning as usual from behind the farmhouse gate, and the chickens scatter in front of them.

To Mark's relief, the regular altar boy has shown up and the service begins without the drama and hilarity of the previous week. The FA Cup is in attendance, but his protruding ears do not seem so funny anymore. In fact, the boys are all a little embarrassed at making fun of this very gentle man, who had greeted them like old friends as they had arrived.

Midway through the service, the congregation stand to read aloud the Nicene Creed, and for the first time, even though he has been attending Mass for as long as he can remember, David actually pays attention to the words, made more powerful in this chanting form:

'We believe in one God, the Father, the Almighty, maker of heaven and earth, of all that is, seen and unseen. We believe in one Lord, Jesus Christ, the only Son of God, eternally begotten of the Father, God from God, Light from Light, true God from true God, begotten, not made, of one Being with the Father. Through him all things were made. For us men and for our salvation he came down from heaven: by the power of the Holy Spirit he became incarnate from the Virgin Mary, and was made man. For our sake he was crucified under Pontius Pilate; he suffered death and was buried. On the third day he rose again in accordance with the Scriptures; he ascended into heaven and is seated at the right hand of the Father. He will come again in glory to judge the living and the dead, and his kingdom will have no end. We believe in the Holy Spirit, the Lord, the giver of life, who proceeds from the Father and the Son. With the Father and the Son he is worshiped and glorified. He has spoken through the Prophets. We believe in one holy catholic and apostolic Church. We acknowledge one baptism for the forgiveness of sins. We look for the resurrection of the dead, and the life of the world to come. Amen.'

Whoa, he thinks. *His kingdom will have no end. If all that is true . . .*

As they sit back down, David looks around at the rest of his family for a reaction and concludes that Mother, Lorraine and Kathy definitely think it is true. *Maybe Father?* The others, not so much.

The highlight of the service is communion. They line up in the aisle behind each other and it is all a bit tight. Lots of 'excuse me's and 'sorry's as the congregation bump and squeeze past each other in the narrow passage: unlike back at their home parish, where they set up in groups along the altar rail – kneeling in wait while the priest goes up the line – parishioners filling in when one leaves (the efficiency and choreography something to be admired). For the boys, communion is a change of pace. A little activity in an otherwise dull ritual of standing, kneeling and sitting on demand. Dissolving the tasteless wafer on their tongues is something to break up the monotony. It also signifies that the service is soon coming to a close and they will be released.

'Let us pray.' The priest finally breaks the silence and they all stand.

'The Lord be with you.'

'And also with you.'

'May almighty God bless you, the Father, and the Son, and the Holy Spirit.'

'Amen.'

'Go in peace, glorifying the Lord by your life.'

'Thanks be to God,' they all respond; Mark a little sarcastically, looking up to the ceiling as he does, then allowing his head to drop back down and letting out a big sigh. Finally, they can get back to the beach.

～～～

They normally like being in the village after Mass, poking about in the shops for a while. But today, because the weather is so nice, they are all quite keen to get back to Whitsands as soon as possible.

On the walk back, the lane becomes very narrow before they reach the farm, and if a car was to pass they would need to make sure they flattened themselves against the high-sided hedgerow.

Suddenly they are aware of something approaching, hidden by the bend in the road. They can hear a couple of raised voices, shouting encouragement. They are met by the farmer coming in the other direction. This is a rare occurrence: having never met him before despite passing through his farm on the public footpaths and narrow country lanes that dissect his property on many occasions. He is slouching along in his Wellington boots, scraping the soles, unable to pick up his feet sufficiently on this inappropriate surface. He is carrying a long wooden staff, dragging it behind him. His pants are held up by braces over a plaid shirt, an olive corduroy bucket hat pulled down low over his head. He does not pause. As he parts through the family, Father wishes him a hearty good morning.

"Ow do. I got 'erd o' bullocks coming up yonder, if you wanna get out the way like.'

They all stop in their tracks to translate what he actually just said, staring at his slowly retreating back, then at each other, then back to where he had just come from.

The first *moo* coincides with the herd coming into view around the corner, the two groups now facing one another. The bullocks are jostling side by side – four or five abreast, ten or twelve rows deep – ambling towards the family, who are momentarily frozen in place. What are they supposed to do? Will the bullocks give way? More of the animals are *moo*ing now, maybe a warning to each other about the obstruction they see ahead. Or like a train's whistle: 'Coming through!'

'Quickly!' orders Father, 'This way everyone!' They turn and hastily follow him back the way they came, overtaking the bemused farmer. Father remembered passing a five-bar gate at the entry to a field, just a short way back. He arrives first, assesses the gate, and starts to climb over, using the horizontal bars like steps on a ladder. The others follow suit, two or three at a time, giggling nervously as the bullocks get closer, with barely a glance from the farmer as he strolls by. Mother is one of the last to arrive and to everyone's surprise she approaches the gate with a curved three-step run-up, placing both hands on the top bar and vaulting it, side-saddle fashion, like a gymnast on the balance beam. She lands safely on the field side, leaving Kevin behind.

'Come on Kevin! Quickly!' his sisters cry out in a mixed anxious chorus. With that, he casually clicks open the latch of the gate and saunters through, snapping the lever shut behind him, just as the herd starts to pass them in a slow, heavy procession. The family watch on in awe of these magnificent beasts, close-up but well out of harm's way; the faces of the smaller children pressing up against the wooden bars of the gate, the older ones and the parents leaning on it. The farmer's son is at the back of the herd and gives them all a casual wave, then slaps the rump of the final bullock to keep it moving along. After they have all passed, Kevin opens the gate and the family pass through, shuffling back into the road, watching as the bullocks are guided into an open field a short way down on the opposite side of the road. With relief they turn and continue on their way, excitedly recounting their versions of the encounter to each other. Someone mentions Mother's impressive leap, and they all burst out laughing.

~~~

This post-church morning marks the beginning of their second week. As they walk back through the farm, they all agree that the second week of the holiday is always the best. They become a little deflated when Kevin points out that it is also the last week of the summer. He tries to cheer them up immediately by reminding them that there are a full six days left yet, or seven more nights. Rather than think in these terms, Mark divides that time into hours, then Peter calculates in his head what that means in minutes.

'That's eight thousand, six hundred and forty minutes.'

Plenty of time.

20.
Tarzan.

Cyril Honey. A name fit for a Hollywood movie star, with heartthrob looks to match. Tanned and muscular, one could imagine him playing the role of Tarzan.

That Sunday afternoon, the beach is busier than normal due to the good weather and an influx of day trippers.

'Would you look at that? The world and Garrett Riley are here today!' No one knows who Mother is referring to when she says this. Just like Janey Mac. Another Irish character. The high tide had sent them packed tightly into the narrow strip of sand that remained. When, eventually, the sea began to give back the beach, the people gradually spread out again, the remains of rounded sandcastles and shallow moats revealed at the retreating water's edge.

It seems like the entire beach community is watching Cyril as he strides down towards the shore. He gives a small wave to a familiar group that he passes, blissfully unaware that he is being generally observed.

It looks like he is going for a swim today, as he has walked beyond his red canoe, which is beached ready to launch at any time. Every day, Cyril would go way out in the bay in his boat to fish with a rod and line, often coming back with an impressive haul of bass or mackerel, which he would clean and gut right there on the beach, before generously dispensing among his seaside neighbours.

He does not pause as he wades further into the water. Ignoring the waves (now breaking around his waist) and the bathers calling to one another, he dives into the crest of the next wave. He swims way out beyond the holidaymakers bobbing about lazily; a perfect Olympian front crawl: his body streamlined flat in the water, a constant flutter kick with his legs, lifting his head alternately left and right to gulp in air every three strokes.

By now, most people on the beach have turned their attention elsewhere. Back to their summer novels, their glossy magazines, or succumbing once again to heavy eyelids. But Father, sat up, hands clasped, his arms linked around his knees, continues to watch as Cyril disappears from view now and again, behind the swell of the waves.

What a guy, he thinks.

With Cyril around everyone on the beach feels safe. It is as if he is the unofficial lifeguard, with all the qualities of Tarzan: enhanced strength, speed, endurance, agility, durability, reflexes, hunter skills. Cyril lives on the beach for the duration of the summer, along with his wife and two young children. Their cottage is the only one right at the base of the cliff, a former boathouse converted into a basic living space. *How far is he going?* wonders Father, craning his neck now to try and locate him.

He has lost sight of him, but then almost immediately spots his prone figure again; much further out now, harder to pick up. He realizes that Cyril is heading towards a pair of big angled rocks, where a flight of cormorants is drying off. Father watches him clamber up the face of one of the rocks, disturbing the resting birds, which immediately unfurl their large wings, take a few running steps and fly away. Cyril carefully crawls up the face of the rock, using his hands to pull himself up the steep angle. He stands tall. Father would not be at all surprised if he suddenly cupped his hands and gave out the jungle yell.

'Yea-ya-ya-ya-ah!'

Instead, Cyril turns to glance back at the beach, then checks for the position of the sun. Next he lays down on his back, stretching out to dry off just like the cormorants, sunbathing a while before tackling the journey back.

In the meantime, Father strolls down to cool off at the water's edge, allowing the surf to lap over his ankles and watching the children splash about around him. A few minutes later, Cyril emerges, coasting in on a breaking wave. He spots Father and heads towards him to strike up a conversation. Aside from the good looks Cyril is a nice person too. Popular and friendly with everyone, always ready to chat. They stand in the water, both with their arms folded, facing out to sea. When Cyril speaks, one realized why he was not a movie star.

'I'll tell yer wot,' he begins in a thick Cornish accent, 'I kent membr s'much mackerel befur! Undruds of'em upalong,' he says, pointing to where he had just been swimming. 'Proper job,' he adds for emphasis.

David comes running out of the water to fetch a floaty board to play with. The Lane family have a number of them and are happy to share.

'Aright, my 'ansum?' asks Cyril, ruffling the boy's hair as he passes by.

Cyril's wife joins them, carrying their son on her hip and holding hands with their daughter. The girl kneels down and starts playing in the shallow water. After a few pleasantries with father, Mrs.Honey hands over the child to Cyril, telling him to keep an eye on them both for a few minutes as she needs to go back to their cottage. He holds the boy up high, arms straight up, giving the youngster a new perspective on life. Then he places him at his feet so that he too can play in the surf. The men continue their conversation, mostly about fishing. At some point, Cyril has an observation about the shifting sands of the beach as it relates to his beach cottage, so both men turn to visualize and gesticulate. What they see is Kathy charging towards them. Both men are a little confused as to why she is sprinting so fast.

'Look out!' says Cyril, playfully.

Kathy dives at his feet and pulls the little boy up and out of the water. He splutters, and there is a delayed reaction before the boy summons up the air in his lungs to let out a massive wail.

'He was face down in the water, I don't think he could get up,' says Kathy strenuously, handing the infant back to a horrified Cyril.

'Oh my godfathers!' he exclaims. 'A'right buy?'

The young boy continues to cry lustily as his mother returns.

'What 'appened?' she asks with concern, taking him back again.

'Oh, 'e just got 'is face wet in the wa'er a bit, e's aright now, int yu buy?'

Kathy walks back to her spot on the beach, a little shaken, then tells her mum what happened.

'I think he was drowning Mum! I was watching them from here, you know, because I babysit for them sometimes, and I noticed him. He sort of flopped forward, probably trying to reach for a shell or something and he just couldn't get up!'

'Heavens!' Mother puts an arm around her visibly upset daughter. 'You will make a great mother one day. How many children do you want?' she asks, trying to diffuse the incident.

Kathy is not sure how to answer that at this moment, so she

part-smiles, part-grimaces at her mother, letting it go.

~~~

She actually would like to have lots of children. But she is torn, even at this young age, because she already knows that she probably will not have any.

Before the summer break, she met with the career counselor at her school: an obligation before entering their fifth year so that they can tailor their subject choices for college or early employment. This all-girls' school is run by Roman Catholic sisters, and the career advice is dispensed by Sister Veronica, a particularly grumpy character from Dublin whom the schoolgirls sarcastically call Sister Sunshine behind her back.

'So, Kathy. What is the plan?' she asks bluntly, leaning forward, elbows planted on the desk, fingers tented.

'Well, I'm going to be a nun. Just like you.'

'Like me? Whoa, whoa, whoa! Hold on there. You cannot just be a nun, young lady. That is not how this works,' she says, showing her palms to Kathy in surrender.

'But I know that's what I want to do. Serve God.'

Sister Veronica removes her glasses and pinches her nose, both to relieve the stress of the spectacles on her face and give her a moment to reflect. No girl has ever walked into her office and told her that she wants to be a nun. Just like her.

'You need to do something else first,' she begins wearily. 'A backup plan of sorts. Something useful. Give yourself time to be sure that you are doing the right thing. You are so young!'

'But—'

'Do you not want to get married? Have children? Do you even like children?'

'I love children.'

Kathy looks down at her hands in her lap.

'Okay. Well, what do you get up to when you are not in school, hmm? Do you have hobbies? What do you do at the weekend, normally?'

She looks up now.

'I love old people too.'

Kathy begins to tell Sister Veronica about St Joseph's, the care home where she has been volunteering for the past year – how she would help serve teas and meals, collect dishes and do the washing-up. She explains how she helps feed the sick ones and make the beds, how she works in the laundry and kitchen, and also spends time in the chapel.

'I like to sit with the residents too, keep them company, just chat really . . .' She realizes that she has been babbling excitedly. The sister has returned her glasses to her face during this time and stares gravely at Kathy, as if she is in trouble.

'How often do you go?'

'Every weekend, unless my mum needs me for something.'

'Sundays?'

'And Saturdays. Oh, and Fridays, after school.'

'Does anyone go with you? A friend, one of your sisters, your mother?'

'No. I go by myself.'

'On the bus?'

'No, I walk.'

'Why do you not get the bus?' she asks, exasperated.

'I don't have any pocket money,' Kathy replies, matter-of-factly.

'Huh,' is all the sister can manage as Kathy looks back down at her hands. After a pause, Sister Veronica looks over Kathy's academic file that she has in front of her. She has also gathered the files of her two older sisters.

'So, Lorraine is going on to teacher training, correct? She wants to teach infants.'

'That's right.'

'And Julie. Let's see, she wants to be a nurse.'

'Yes.'

Sister Veronica looks at Kathy over the top of her glasses.

'Well, I think that is what you should do too.'

'Teaching?'

'What? No! Nursing! Train to be a nurse, like your sister. You will be a more useful nun if you are a qualified nurse. That is if you still want to be one by then,' she adds skeptically, making a note in her file. Kathy sits quietly, contemplating. Sister Veronica looks up, almost surprised that Kathy is still sat there.

'Anything else?' she asks.

'Em, no, Sister.'

'Okay. Good. Nursing it is. Off you go now.' She dismisses Kathy with a wave of her hand. 'Send the next one in, will you?'

'Yes Sister. Thank you, Sister.'

She looks up again only as Kathy has turned to leave the room.

She sits back in her chair and makes the sign of the cross. Then adds 'Future Head Girl?' to her notes.

21.
A Bucket of Water.

Returning to Ferndale that evening, following the fresh air of a full day spent on the beach, it feels a little musty in the sitting room. They are all giddy from the activities of the afternoon – a proper time having been had by all. They are sun- and wind-swept, that warm feeling staying with them as the setting sun beats through the picture window overlooking the sea. Soon, their minds are peaceful and drowsy. Some are too tired to move.

In the kitchen, Mother has cleared away just enough counter space to roll out some pastry. She is going to make a family favourite dessert: lemon meringue pie. Her wedding ring clicks against the rolling pin with each push. The lemon filling of sugar, flour, cornstarch, lemon juice and egg yolks is already prepared in a saucepan. She has enlisted David to vigorously whisk the egg whites for the meringue: a chore he is attacking earnestly, pacing up and down the path outside the kitchen, switching arms every now and again to relieve the ache. Mother notices him passing the window back and forwards as she drapes the pastry over the rolling pin to lay it into the dish. She scissors the extra dough away from the edges and pricks the layer all over with a fork. Normally, at home, she would put this in the fridge to rest, but at Whitsands her only option is to set it in the cold cupboard outside.

'Nearly there,' she encourages David as she passes him with the pie crust, 'just a little longer, stiff peaks remember. You should be able to turn it upside down.'

David is tempted to try that experiment straight away, but he knows the meringue is not quite ready for that yet.

While the pie is resting, Mother gathers the leftover dough and forms it into a new ball and starts rolling it out again with a liberal dusting of flour.

Click, click, click, goes her wedding band.

Once she is satisfied with the thickness, she searches the shelves for an appropriately sized circle to use as a cutter. She selects a plastic beaker about four inches in diameter and pushes it into the dough a dozen times, forming twelve even circles with minimal waste. On a lower shelf she locates a couple of baking trays.

David returns to the kitchen, mischievously turning the bowl upside down over his head.

'Oh David, be careful!'

'Are you making jam tarts too?' he asks, setting the bowl down.

'That's right. Fetch the jam would you. Oh, and a teaspoon.'

Once the round tarts are filled, Mother gathers the remaining dough, picking off little pieces and rolling them on her palm into balls the size of peas. She places these in the centre of each tart.

'Why do you do that?' David asks watching her.

'Waste not, want not.'

David shrugs. She puts the pie and the tarts in the oven and turns her attention to the main course. Tonight, they are having Scotch eggs. The eggs have already been hard-boiled and peeled and are now cooling in a bowl. The sausage meat, along with some Worcestershire sauce, mustard and sage, had been prepared and mixed together in a bowl earlier in the day to save time. David's next task is to divide the filling evenly between twelve, then wrap it around each of the dozen boiled eggs. Mother sets up an assembly line of three bowls of flour, beaten egg and breadcrumbs. She coats each meat-covered egg in the flour, dips them in the egg mixture, then dredges each in breadcrumbs. Ten minutes later, a dozen crisp, golden orbs of beauty are plucked from the oven to cool.

Meantime David is helping with the salad – chopping cucumbers into large chunks and tomatoes into quarters.

Everyone is ravenous and devours them quickly. Mother has anticipated that Father, and probably Mark too, would want more than just one, but they are not the only ones tonight after such an active day, so she divides the additional Scotch eggs into eight quarters and shares them out, Mother and Lorraine declining an extra portion.

~~~

After tea, Julie clears away the table, while Peter sets about heating up some water in saucepans on the stove to do the washing-up. Meanwhile, Kevin, the eldest, steps out of the kitchen door and heads around the back of the house, carrying the butter and milk back to the cold storage. He puts them away then notices the spigot where they wash the sand off their feet before entering the house. Next to it is a bucket. He has an idea. He fills the bucket half-full of water, then takes it around to the front of the house, secretly placing it on the veranda in front of the living room, beneath the window. He picks up a garden chair off the grass and slides it in place next to the bucket, then heads back inside.

By the time all the dishes have been put away it is twilight and everyone is gathered in the sitting room, settling into their evenings. Kevin pops his head around the door.

'I'm just going for a quick swim,' he announces to their surprise, then disappears before anyone can either go with him or ask questions.

'He's not really going for a swim, is he?' asks Lorraine, 'He's just had tea!'

'He hasn't had pudding yet!'

The others shrug and look equally puzzled.

'He'll be OK, it's been more than half an hour,' says Father.

'What does that mean?' asks Martin.

'We did this in Human Biology last term.' Julie is quick to share her new-found knowledge. 'His blood is working to digest his tea, which means his legs and arms won't get enough blood to function properly. He could drown!'

'He won't drown,' reassures Father.

A few seconds later, Kathy spots a snorkel passing along the front of the window.

'What's that?' she asks, just as it goes out of sight.

'What's what?' says Peter, looking up from his comic.

'There it is again!'

The snorkel glides back the other way. Now they are all transfixed by the scene in the window. It goes by two more times, perfectly aligned so that the top of it breaks over the horizon. On the third pass it stops in the middle and begins to rise. First, they see the unmistakable mop of fair hair that belongs to Kevin, then his face slowly surfaces. He is wearing goggles. He moves about in slow motion, as if underwater, much to the amusement of the family. His cheeks are puffing in and out, taking in oxygen. He waves slowly at them, they wave back, and he floats by past the edge of the window. They keep watching, expecting more, and sure enough, a few seconds later, Kevin returns. He is walking and leaning backwards, doing the backstroke. Once again, he goes beyond the window, then returns the other way. When he comes back again, he is underwater, this time without the snorkel and goggles. He is holding his breath, cheeks full. He waves slowly again at the grinning faces on the other side of the glass. He rises up, appearing to break the sea's horizon; as he surfaces, he tilts his head back and spits out a fountain of water, before dipping down and out of sight. The family are in stitches. His grand finale is a leap from the chair, passing through the frame of the window, clutching his nose. He is gone for a few seconds – some of the children move to get a closer look – when suddenly a deluge of water slams against the window, startling them, making them flinch, then laugh uncontrollably as they get the joke. While they are still recovering and checking the window, hoping for an encore, Kevin walks back in the room with a towel draped over his shoulder.

'Well that was refreshing,' he says, to more raucous laughter.

22.
A Dish Rack.

Many of the convenience foods that Mother served the
family were the result of restrictions that were in place during
World War Two and for many years after. Back then, butter,
sugar, meat, tea, jam, biscuits, breakfast cereals, cheese, eggs
and milk were all rationed. Fields were ploughed to grow wheat
and potatoes. Tins of spam and corned beef, condensed milk and
dried eggs were pantry staples. It was around this time that
the frozen ready-to-cook fish finger was introduced. There
are twenty fish fingers to a box, which works out to be two
per person in this family. The processed fish stick, wrapped
in breadcrumbs, weighs just one ounce. It is half an inch thick,
one and a half inches wide and four and a half inches long, which
works out to be around three to four bites per person. Not enough

for Mark. He is a growing teenager, he could eat most of his meals all over again. If he had studied the packaging he would have realized that the box of twenty contained five portions, or four fish fingers per person. Mother knows this, but feeding eight growing children and a husband on a small budget is challenging. Potatoes and a bag of frozen peas are relatively cheap, so they fill out the plate. A little dollop of tartar sauce from a jar gives it a more sophisticated air. Slices of buttered white bread are considered a side dish, some of the children make chip butties with them. A pot of tea is the accompanying beverage.

'Well I've done my bit, who's on dishes?' Mother sits back, the aftermath of the meal in front of them.

〜〜

There are still chores to be done, all those little things that come with you on a holiday that seem to get in the way. The family have devised a fair way of dividing housework, what they refer to as 'The Joy List' – so named as an intention to make them feel that is for the benefit of all of them and so should be undertaken gladly, rather than what it really is: a duty. Kevin is in charge of figuring out who does what and when, producing a drawn-up diagram on a sheet of paper that he Sellotapes to the inside of the pantry door, writing up a new one every Sunday night to rotate the roster. The same applies here at Whitsands. He starts by listing the chores in a column on the left side of the page in shorthand, as they all know what it involves:

Breakfast: set & clear (which includes opening up the table leaves to its full size; laying the tablecloth; setting out plates, bowls, teacups with saucers and cutlery; pulling out cereal boxes and the glass sugar bowl from the sideboard; fetching the butter, milk, marmalade and jam from the cold storage outside; then clearing everything away after, followed by sweeping up crumbs and running the carpet sweeper around the front room and hallway),

Breakfast: wash (first boiling the water on the stovetop),

Breakfast: dry (which also means putting all the dishes away),

Shop (a daily requirement to stock up on groceries – requiring a couple of them, in order to help carry all the foodstuffs),

Dinner (an assistant to Mother to help prepare sandwiches, dilute the concentrated fruit drinks, collect packets of crisps, and – on a sunny day – carry the holdall down to the beach),

Tea: set & clear,

Tea: wash,

Tea: dry, which rounded out the daily duties.

Kevin would write in the days of the week across the top of the page and then fill in the rows with numbers one to eight in pencil, checking first that it worked out fairly before over-writing the numbers with names in pen (one being the eldest, eight the youngest). He was happy to see that, here at Whitsands, it worked out each child would have two days off during the week. No one complained; sometimes they would negotiate between themselves to swop duties depending on the activities of the day, or volunteer to do the grocery shopping because they had run out of sweets and needed to view their options. Mother prepared the meals and Father was able to relax away from his normal duty of washing and drying the dishes at home every day.

~~~

Mark, a little reluctantly, starts stacking the dirty plates: collecting the knives and forks on the top plate and sliding the next one passed to him under the bottom of the pile. Kevin joins him in the kitchen: filling a kettle with cold water, lighting a ring on the stove and setting it to boil. As they wait for the water to heat up they both clear away the rest of the table: cups and saucers for washing, returning the butter and milk to the cold cupboard. Mark wipes down the dining table, collecting crumbs in the palm of his hand. One leaf is folded away to open up the space for the evening's entertainment, perhaps a game of Gin Rummy or Scrabble, yet to be determined. Lorraine runs the sweeper, even though it is not her job today.

Kevin is back in the kitchen, donning the rubber Marigold gloves. Mark strips the tea towel from the rail with a flick of his wrist and begins wiping the first plate dry and setting it straight back on the open shelf on top of the unused plates. The kitchen door is wide open, both for light and airflow from the warm kitchen. It is still light outside, only six thirty, three more hours before sunset at this time of year.

Mark hears them coming before he sees them, their chatter and quick footfalls announcing their enthusiastic approach down the curved path that leads to the back of the house. Simon and Paul Lane bounce down the final steps and breathlessly frame the doorway.

'Hiya. Coming down to the beach? The tide's way out, we could kick a ball about, or play some cricket?'

'OK,' says Mark, the chance to kick a ball never turned down. 'I've got to dry the tea dishes first though.'

'Tea?' asks Paul.

'Yeah, we just had tea. We could see you down there if you like.'

'What did you have?' asks Simon.

'Fish fingers, chips and peas.'

'That's not tea! That's supper,' Paul scoffs.

'Or you could call it dinner I suppose,' adds Simon.

Kevin laughs, 'We had dinner on the beach.'

'What did you have?' asks Simon again.

'Cheese and pickle sandwiches, crisps, Ribena, KitKats.'

'That's not dinner! That's lunch!'

Mark shrugs, 'Well, we call it dinner.'

'OK, but why are you drying the dishes?' asks Simon incredulously.

'What do you mean?' The question makes no sense to Kevin, pausing his scrubbing to look directly at the two boys.

'We don't do that.'

'We've got a dish rack,' says the other one with a swagger, 'you just stack up the dishes and let them dry themselves.'

Mark feels as if this is another example of the perceived superiority that the Lanes have over his family. They own their own bungalow. Their parents are both teachers. They have a car. They call it lunch. And now, they have a dish rack.

Kevin considers defending themselves by reminding the Lane boys that this is not their bungalow, but he knows that they do not have a dish rack at home either. It might also open up yet another opportunity for Simon to let them know that they own theirs. But before he can say anything Mark dismisses them.

'We'll see you down there,' he tells them flatly, turning away to select the next plate for drying. He vows to make them pay for their aloofness on the beach. He will show them who is better with a football at his feet.

~~~

All the children head down the cliff for some bonus beach time. Mark is carrying the plastic football in the style of Bobby Moore, the England World Cup captain. He has it casually trapped between his hip and wrist. It is still rankling him that there is obviously a class divide between the two families. Everyone he knows calls the midday meal dinner.

Why don't we call it lunch?

Then he has a thought.

'They're wrong!' he shouts over his shoulder to his older brother.

'Who's wrong?'

'The Lanes. About dinner.'

'How come?'

'If it's called lunch then why do we have school dinners?'

Kevin thinks about this and expands the argument.

'And dinner ladies!'

'See!'

Suddenly Mark cannot wait to correct them. He starts to sing a familiar refrain to the nursery rhyme melody of 'Frère Jacques':

'School dinners, school dinners,

stringy meat, stringy meat,

sloppy semolina, sloppy semolina,

that's what we, get to eat.'

His brothers and sisters all join in, repeating it over and over again until they reach the beach, gleefully sprinting on to the soft sand to join the misinformed Lane boys.

They end up playing a rare game of family versus family, the three Lane boys – Chris, Simon and Paul – versus Mark, David and Peter. Short piles of hand-formed sand for goalposts, a dragged heel for the goal lines.

It is soon obvious that the Lane family are being outclassed. They are finding it difficult to retain possession, let alone have a chance to score. At one point, David skillfully feigns to go one way with a drop of his shoulder, sending Chris Lane the wrong way, pushing the ball ahead as he sprints away. Chris makes up a little of the ground between them, sufficient enough to lunge at him from behind and recklessly scythe him down. David crashes to the sand and immediately grabs for his sore shin. He sits up and rubs it furiously to dim the pain. Meanwhile, Chris is unrepentant and dribbles the ball away to start a counter-attack.

Mark is not having it and stops his progress by easily tackling him head-on, then picking up the ball.

'That was a foul.'

'Come on, it wasn't that bad. Look he's okay.'

David has got to his feet but bends over to continue to rub his shin.

'Foul,' repeats Mark simply, acting like a referee.

'He just can't take it. That's how Norman Hunter plays.'

You can tell a lot about someone by their nickname. Leeds United's legendary defender Norman Hunter was fondly known as Norman 'Bites Yer Legs' Hunter, in reference to his combative, physical style of play.

'Well you're not Norman Hunter. You're rubbish at football.'

Chris has nothing to say to that and decides he has had enough. With a dismissive flap of his arm he walks off. The game is over as far as the Lane boys are concerned, and the other two follow him.

'We win then,' says Peter, volunteering to go in goal for crosses and headers with his two brothers.

When they begin to lose the light, David suggests one more goal before they pack up. It takes them another fifteen minutes of near misses, fluffed crosses, misdirected headers and spectacular saves, before Mark, having had enough, blasts a volley past a stationary Peter from close range.

'I'm not getting that.' Peter turns away, trudging up the beach.

It is so dark now that Mark has difficulty finding the

orange-coloured football. David helps him look for it and they finally spot it nestled among a small group of rocks. They jog to catch up with Peter, who is already on the cliff path, using the meagre remaining light to stumble home together.

23.
The Black Sheep.

At breakfast the next morning, Mark brings up the conversation with Father that he had with Simon on the beach the night before.

'So, Simon says they don't have dinner at school, he says they call it lunch.'

'"Simon says, Simon says" . . .' mocks Julie.

Mark continues undeterred, 'And they don't have dinner ladies either, they call them lunch ladies.'

'Same thing,' Father reaches for the jam and drops an extravagant blob on the side of his plate, 'the Lanes go to a posh school, that's all.'

Mark is not convinced.

'Then how come they play football at his school, not rugby?'

Father eyes him over his teacup as he takes a swig.

'Okay, that's enough. Aren't you on shopping today? You better go and see your mother for the list.'

~~~

Mark has held a grudge for three years now; bitter at being sent to the same school as his older brother. A very well-respected institution, but one that played rugby rather than football. The school preferred rugby because they believed its values were those they wished to instill in their boys: teamwork, respect, enjoyment, discipline, sportsmanship. As the saying goes, *Rugby puts hairs on your chest.* But Mark prefers the simplicity of football. The game affords him the chance to be more creative and expressive, with less of a structure than rugby.

Kevin really could not care less about the sporting options, but to Mark it feels like a life-or-death decision, being denied his one real passion as an eleven year old. He excels at it, even has aspirations to play professionally, as many boys of his age do. He has talent, which he feels is being wasted playing rugby. Dad had proudly watched him play for Plymouth Schoolboys versus local rivals Exeter a few years before, Mark gleefully tormenting the opposition left-back as they thrashed them three-nil. On the bus on the way home he had pleaded his case for going to a different school. His parents were sympathetic, but the other school was not as well regarded academically, so the decision was made. Mother and Father had finished their schooling prematurely because of World War Two, so they valued the education of their children highly. Although Mother was christened Emily Christine she was known from an early age as Bunty, having been an avid reader of the popular weekly girls' comic of the same name. Her favourite stories were 'Bella of Bonnybanks School', about a princess who attended the exclusive girls' boarding school; and 'Supergirl', the adventures of a bionic schoolgirl, Susie Sullivan. So, when she was taken out of her school at twelve years old, she was devastated, spending the rest of her school-age years helping her mother with housework, full of regret.

But Mark was not happy.

~~~

He is shopping with Martin today; they don't need much, he could manage alone, but Martin insists on tagging along. There are only five items on the list, which Mark has folded up, along with a one-pound note, and stuffed into his pocket.

'Wait for me!' Martin cries out, as he is still putting on his sandals by the kitchen door when Mark sets off up the path already.

'It's just not fair,' Mark complains over his shoulder as Martin catches up, settling in behind him in single file.

'What's not fair?'

'School. Rugby. Football.' He spits out as an answer.

'Oh.'

'They make me play for the school rugby team so I can't play football on Saturdays.'

~~~

He tended to take out his aggression on his younger brothers – Peter being a particular target of his – playing rough, acting brash and boastful, making them feel weak and lesser than him. One day, in an attempt to harness this new-found anger, Father brought home two pairs of second-hand boxing gloves, sparring a little with his son to teach him the basics. Father had been school champion, so knew the benefits of letting off steam productively. Which worked, to a degree. None of his brothers were willing to take him on, so he beat up most of his friends in a makeshift ring in the back garden.

~~~

Martin has been thinking as they make their way up towards the cliff road.

'Why don't you just be rubbish?'

'What?'

'At rugby I mean. Why don't you just play rubbish? You know, drop the ball all the time, don't tackle anyone, miss all your kicks. That's what I'd do. Or probably will do if they pick me. I don't like rugby either.'

'And then they wouldn't pick me for the team.'

'Yep.'

That was not in Mark's competitive nature, so he had to admit, 'Huh. Hadn't thought of that . . .'

Whitsands calmed him. He loved the loose-style pickup games of football on the beach when the tide was low. Barefoot. Cricket stumps or jumpers for goalposts. Anyone was welcome to join in: participation was requested by walking onto the 'field' with a raised hand, enquiring without words which way they were kicking. Taking into account the balance of the play and the age range and number of players per team, they would be assigned a direction to play towards by a more senior member of the original party; normally Mark, unless he was too busy dribbling through the opposition defence to notice.

~~~

When they reach Bellamy's Cafe, he pulls out the list as Martin goes in search of a packet of Rolos. He unfurls the list and circles around the shop, loading his basket.

A pint of milk.

Cornflakes.

Butter.

A loaf of Mother's Pride, thick slice.

Newspaper.

At the checkout, Mrs Bellamy rings him up. She glances at Mark over the top of her glasses as he stands in front of her with his banknote ready. She knows the family, they come here every summer for a fortnight in August. They get letters sometimes.

Ten of 'em. And this is all they buy from me?

'What are you living on down there, fresh air sandwiches?'

Mark is horrified. It makes him feel ashamed. As if his family are starving and cannot even afford to eat. He stammers a quiet, indignant response.

'No.'

161

'Hmm. Here's your change. See you tomorrow,' she adds sarcastically.

On the way out, Mark turns to Martin and whispers.

'Did you hear that? Fresh air sandwiches!'

'Is that funny? What does it mean?'

'She thinks we're poor.'

'Are we?'

'Not really.'

'Fresh air sandwiches,' repeats Martin, 'I still don't get it.'

Mark explains:

'She thinks that we can't afford to buy stuff for our sandwiches from her shop.'

'Oh. Well, Kathy says that it's expensive at Mrs Bellamy's compared to back home. That's why we brought all that stuff with us. Mum's smart.'

This realization makes Mark feel a lot better.

'Come on, let's run back. The tide's out already!'

24.
A Bump in the Night.

'They had not gone up more than a dozen steps when they both simultaneously stopped to listen, looking into each other's eyes with a new apprehension across the flickering candle flame. From the room they had left hardly ten seconds before came the sound of doors quietly closing. It was beyond all question; they heard the booming noise that accompanies the shutting of heavy doors, followed by the sharp catching of the latch.'

David clicks off his torch, convinced that he heard something outside. He rests his book on his chest, a classic horror story by

Algernon Blackwood called *The Empty House*. He listens hard for the telltale signs of the bogeyman, lurking in the shadows. There is a strong wind up tonight. The house is creaking and branches occasionally scratch against their bedroom window. The sounds of the crashing waves from the beach below disguise the movements of the monster. David is convinced that it is lurking at the corner of the house. By the kitchen. Near the door.

Is it locked? he wonders, also questioning his desire to read horror stories at night.

~~~

'The scarier the better,' he bragged when they made their selections at the library the week before. The children all love going to the library. Not just for the reading material, but because their local library is located in the grounds of a former fort. They imagine a portcullis dropping down behind them as they enter through the gatehouse to skip across the parade ground; passing by battlements, watchtowers, cannon mounts and turrets. Their imagination is engaged before they even get into the building.

~~~

Martin has a Hardy Boys mystery on the go, he's reading *The Missing Chums,* but he prefers his collection of *Peanuts* paperback books last thing at night, a stack of them on the floor next to his bed. When David switches his torch off, Martin decides he should do the same, placing *Who Do You Think You Are, Charlie Brown?* on the top of the pile.

Peter had long ago put down his P. G. Wodehouse novel, *Eggs,*

Beans and Crumpets, only managing a couple of pages before flicking off his torch and going to sleep.

Mark did not read anything tonight, exhausted from playing football on the beach all day.

The isolation of the bungalow makes David a prime victim. Of course, the intruder would choose a moonless, windy night like tonight to plan his attack. It is so dark. And he is feeling especially vulnerable on the bottom bunk, closest to the door. Within easy reach. Yet he is somewhat comforted by having his three brothers sleeping in the same room with him.

'Did anyone hear that?' David whispers, as the same branch scratches at the window.

'It's just a branch, go to sleep,' assures Peter, drowsily.

David makes a mental note to check the surrounding bushes in the morning to see if it could possibly be foliage causing his unrest, as his older brother claims. If he survives the night, that is. He lies there, hands behind his head. Eyes wide open. Senses alert. When suddenly, as if to prove his point, there is an enormous crash from the other bedroom, which makes the whole house shake.

Father arrives in the hallway first, carrying his torch. The four boys only then getting to open their door and peer out from behind each other, not committing to go any further just yet. Father ignores them and quickly turns the handle of the girls' bedroom door and enters, not knowing what he might be walking into.

'I'm okay,' assures Kathy, sitting on the floor. Father shines the light on her face, she puts up her arm to shield it from the glare.

'What happened?' he asks, bending down to comfort her. The other girls are sat up in their beds on their elbows, looking scared, mouths wide open. The five boys are all at the door now.

'I fell out of bed,' she says quietly, a little embarrassed.

'What happened?' asks Mother from the back of the group, missing the explanation as she pushes the boys forward so that the entire family all shuffle into the small room.

'She fell out of bed,' says Father. 'Are you sure you're okay?' he asks, kneeling next to her and checking her over. She nods earnestly. There is a moment of silence as they all take in the distance. Father directs the light up to the now empty top bed of the triple-bunk, and then slowly back down to Kathy, assessing the height from which she had plummeted. Amid a few gasps and mutterings, the shock on Kathy's face suddenly gives way to a broad grin as she announces loudly, 'I fell out of bed!' And then her unmistakable laugh fills the room.

'I fell out of bed!' she repeats for the third time, as the rest of the family start to see the funny side; some joining in with the laughter, others not yet quite convinced that it was something to laugh about.

'Okay,' says Father, helping Kathy to her feet, 'nobody's hurt, calm down now. Let's all go back to bed.'

Mother stays behind to further check on Kathy, to tuck her in like she used to do when she was a little girl. Satisfied that she is unharmed, she says goodnight to all the girls and heads back to bed.

~~~

The boys are all wide awake now, so David has a request.

'Hey, Pete. Tell us one of your stories.'

Peter has a knack for making up stuff: imaginative tales that even he does not know where they will lead. He has been writing a book of sorts with his best friend at school, Mark Wheeler. The pair share a desk together in class and are usually scribbling ideas to each other back and forth, rather than paying attention. Although they both somehow manage to pass all their subjects. Their private endeavour is descriptively titled *The Little Red Book with the Red Bit Down the Side*: an exercise in competitive creative writing, edited by their alter egos, Dan and Bob Runks. It contains silly short stories, whimsical line drawings, pasted comic strips with altered captions and ludicrous sports reports. There are two recurring characters throughout: Whimsey Trusset and Kenneth Whopplespoon.

~~~

'Okay,' Peter sighs reluctantly. He is reminded of how, earlier in the day, David had trapped a housefly against the window in his cupped hand and taken it to a spider's web in a hedge on the beach path.

'Welcome to the Late-Night-On-The-Fly News,' Peter begins in the style of a news show host. 'The top story tonight may be distressing for some viewers, coming to us from Whitsand Bay in

Cornwall. Over to, em, over to Phil, our fly-on-the-wall reporter.'

Peter changes his voice to a higher, more excited tone. 'Thanks, Fred. Yes, witnesses are coming forward here today describing the shocking actions of a young, some say immature human being this morning.'

David has a sense of where this is going. His curiosity about spiders, black beetles, grasshoppers, sandflies, slow worms or butterflies has not gone unnoticed.

'Apparently, this terrible young person caught one of our own bare-handed and proceeded to feed him to a spider. That's right, he actually threw the fly directly onto the spider's web, with obvious consequences. By all accounts, this terrible boy stood and watched the ensuing feeding frenzy unfold. None of us feel safe here. Back to you in the studio.'

Peter continues in the other voice, 'Thanks for that update Frank. It just goes to show how careful we all have to be out there, especially when we keep banging and banging and banging our heads against this strange, invisible force, never getting anywhere, whatever that is . . . Anyway, remember flies, if at first you don't succeed, turn around and just fly the other way. And that's the news on the fly. Goodnight all. Sleep tight. Don't let the bedbugs bite.'

'Goodnight,' each of them reply, grinning in the dark.

25.
Main Beach.

By Tuesday, the weather reverted back to being dull and cloudy, which had them all worried that they would not see the sun again for the rest of the week. The good weather at the start of this second week had made the days linger almost endlessly. It somehow made them feel that they had been at the seaside for weeks already. There are still four clear days left to go, but now the end is in sight. Time is gathering speed.

After breakfast, Mother has a suggestion.

'Shall we all walk over to Main Beach? The tide's way out.' Tregantle Beach, otherwise known as Main Beach, is popular with day trippers because of its shallower access from the cliff top and ample free parking available in an adjacent open field. It also has a cafe directly on the beach, selling ice creams, tea, sweets, and trays of chips with packets of tomato sauce. It has a popular bathroom, too, which allows the holidaymakers to linger longer.

Although the sea is murmuring a long way out, by the time the family arrive down on their beach the tide has already turned. There are not many people about, the low grey sky and the cry of gulls adding to the feeling of bleakness.

The distance to Main beach is about a mile and a half, which should take them about twenty minutes. Kathy is in a little discomfort, although she would not admit it. The fall from the top bunk during the night was more painful than she had first realized, so she settles in next to her mum, linking arms. Lorraine notices and moves to her mother's other side to link with her too. Soon, the three of them are walking in step, which reminds Mother of a verse that her own mother would recite to her when she was a little girl. It was a marching rhyme in time with their steps, to encourage her to keep going when she was getting tired.

'Left, right, left.
Left. Left. Left.
I had a good friend and he left.
He left because he thought he was right.
Left, right, left.
Left. Left. Left.'

The girls are familiar with this and join in immediately, happily repeating it over and over together.

The boys are kicking a ball to each other as they jog along. Father would occasionally join in, if the ball happened to come his way. He had a distinctive technique – a short backlift with no follow-through, striking the ball with the top part of his foot, knee over the ball – resulting in an accurate, though unspectacular pass. He had suffered a broken right leg during a game as a young man, so his football days were cut short, and he was still cautious in these later years not to exert that limb.

David and Julie are lagging behind the rest; digging up the sand with their bare feet near the shoreline, spotting air bubbles as the water recedes in search of clams that they feel are burrowing just below the surface. There are a few empty razor clam shells around, pecked clean by the seagulls, the sight of them encouraging their exploration.

Main Beach is noticeable because of a huge rock, shaped like an acute triangle. A flat, crawlable side slopes towards the point at roughly forty-five degrees; the other side is steeper and shorter, craggy and climbable. The rock sits by itself in the middle of the beach when the tide is fully out, but gets mostly covered when the tide is in. A flagpole has been drilled into the peak of the rock, a large red flag displaying when the water is deemed unsafe for swimming.

The sight of it in the distance is the family's landmark. When they first spot the rock, it looks small and still a long way away. For a while, it seems that it is not getting any closer, until eventually it appears to be within striking distance and the more energetic of them sprint towards its base, then race towards the top. Mark gets there first. The three younger boys follow by age and they all breathlessly take in the elevated view before them.

'The tide's coming in,' notices Peter as the water laps against the furthermost point of their rocky vantage view.

'It's been coming in for a while now,' says David.

'Should we be going back then?' asks Martin, nervously looking back towards their beach. They are all aware of the chance of a tidal cut-off.

'Plenty of time,' says Mark, 'look they're going to get ice creams. Come on!'

~~~

Whitsand Bay has about a dozen coves, shaped on either side by tall rock features that get cut off from each other by the high tide. Over the course of a fortnight, the family will experience the tides through a full cycle of time. When they arrived early afternoon on the Saturday, they could see from Ferndale that the tide was about halfway out, and within fifteen minutes or so of observation they determined that it was on its way in. When they got up on Sunday morning for the walk to church in Millbrook, they noticed that the tide was far out, which was disappointing, because they knew that by the time they returned some four hours later (a two-mile walk there; the service; shopping in the village afterwards; the walk back; then a quick sandwich at the cottage) the waves would be crashing high on the rocks, and there would be no beach in sight until at least four in the afternoon.

~~~

The boys scamper down the rock and catch up with the others as they reach the steps outside the cafe.

'Ninety-nines all round?' asks Father to gleeful shrieks, a rare treat. He goes inside to place the order while the family commandeer two picnic benches adjacent to the entrance. No one thinks to give Father a hand with the ten cones he is about to receive, each filled with a swirl of soft vanilla ice cream and a Cadbury's chocolate flake pressed into it. However, the cafe is familiar to large orders like this one. They have a customized solution for transporting these delicate structures. They have crafted a number of containers out of lightweight balsa wood, neatly stacked on the counter at the back of the room: each a twelve-inch square base with sixteen even compartments, three and a half inches high.

One attendant dispenses the ice cream into the cone, then hands it off to another. She then adds the finger of crumbly chocolate and stands it snugly in the container. They repeat this process nine more times. As the girl processes the transaction at the till, she requests that Father returns the container before he leaves.

'Genius,' he says, handing over the payment and taking it from them.

'Genius,' agrees Kevin, first to notice the arrangement as Father appears.

They lose themselves for a few minutes, quietly relishing the moment. Even the sun has glimpsed through the clouds. Father turns his face up to meet it, eyes closed.

'Scrumptious.' Kathy, first to finish, breaks the silence and licks her lips.

Mother sighs contentedly.

'Shouldn't we be getting back, the tide's coming in quite fast,' notices Julie.

'Oh, save us and keep us!' exclaims Mother, quickly getting to her feet.

The return pace is quicker than the amble outward, more of a direct line than a meandering exploration. Some are a little anxious about being caught out by the tide; the boys a little less concerned because they know they can confidently scramble across the rocks if necessary.

The two eldest girls and Father arrive back at their beach first, wading through calf-high surf and small breaking waves at the final rocky point. They move towards the back of the beach and rest on the rocks to wait for the others. It is another three minutes before they spot the four boys clambering over the rocks towards them, revelling in the sport of it all.

'Where's Mum?' Julie asks them nervously as they approach.

Father appeases her:

'She'll be here soon enough. Don't worry, Kathy and Kevin are with her.'

Sure enough, Lorraine sees them first, wading through the water, now almost waist high.

'Here they are!'

It is evident that they are perfectly happy, even exhilarated, from the adventure.

'I was worried that you were going to get stranded,' admits Julie.

Kevin has a ready response.

'We sent Kathy through first. She's the shortest; so if she made it we knew we'd be okay.'

They all laugh, then Kevin looks back around where they had come from and raises his forefinger, as if he is missing something.

'I meant to go to the loo,' he quips, 'I'd better go back.' With that he turns and feigns to set off.

'Eejit!' says Mother, laughing with them all.

26.
Cascade.

The appeal of a trip over to the peaceful village of Cawsand should have been due to its pleasant shingle beach, with rock pools and inlets. Or the fact that the village has hardly changed for centuries, with its tiny, pastel-coloured cottages spilling down towards the sheltered harbour. Not changed, that is, apart from the smuggling. It was once a hotbed for smugglers, who used Cawsand as a port-of-call for the contraband liquor they brought ashore. For David and Martin, when the family would pick the day that they would catch the double-decker bus to Cawsand, it meant just one thing. Something that they hoped would still be there. They had discovered it the previous year, when the country was still getting used to its new currency. On Valentine's Day of that year, there were twelve pennies to the shilling and twenty shillings to the pound. The following day all that was history and the pound was now made up of one hundred new pence. Decimalization meant old coins were being phased out and new ones introduced. They had been using the new five pence, ten pence and fifty pence coins for a couple of years already, brought in alongside the thruppenny bit, the sixpence, the shilling and the ten-bob note. When it became official on February fifteenth, the half-pence, one pence and two pence coins were introduced. Banks were closed for four days from the previous Thursday to prepare for the changeover.

The boys took to it quickly. It made much more sense to them than the old system. The first thing they did with their shiny new coins was to go down to the sweet shop. The owner was struggling to get to grips with it all. He could still accept the old money before it was to be phased out: sixpence was worth two and a half pence of the new money, twelve pence equaled a shilling. There were jars of sweets on shelves behind the counter, and David asked for two ounces of his favourite, bonbons: small toffee bites dusted in powdered sugar. They would normally cost him sixpence. As the shopkeep unscrewed the jar and shook out the sweets onto the scale, they could see how he paused between the shakes, that he was deep in thought, calculating the price in his head.

'That'll be two new pence, or sixpence,' he says, pouring the bonbons into a conical paper sleeve, twisting the top to seal it, as he handed it over to David, who in exchange handed him the requested newly minted coin. The boys were delighted that, for now, their confectionary was cheaper than yesterday.

~~~

'Two adults and eight halves for Cawsand, please,' says Father to the driver as the family pile on behind him and head straight up the stairs.

It is an exciting bus ride. They have the top deck virtually to themselves (apart from an older couple towards the back), the family taking up the front three rows. The two youngest boys stand at the window: holding onto the rail in front of them for balance, riding along like surfers, bending their knees to absorb the bumps and leaning into the hairpin turns. Mother warns them to be careful, but they are having too much fun. They cannot believe that this is a legitimate bus route: the lanes are so narrow at some parts that the bus would *thwack* into the upper branches of the trees, causing David and Martin to flinch and duck. The driver is obviously enjoying himself, confident almost to the point of recklessness, flinging the bus about as if it were a much smaller vehicle. If a car were to come in the opposite direction, surely they would be stuck, the boys reckoned. Luckily, none do, and the driver eases off as they descend into the village itself.

After a short walk through the winding streets, the family camp out on the beach.

'We're going to the fish and chip shop,' announces David immediately, as he and Martin stand around on the edge of the rest of the group, who have all sat down.

'Why? We're going to get pasties later,' says Mother.

'We're not buying anything.'

'Then why are you going to the fish and chip shop?'

David hesitates, a little embarrassed.

'Well, there's this game . . .'

~~~

A Drop Case machine is one in which the coin itself is used as the projectile, rather than the more usual ball bearing. The Cascade is such a machine, and the boys are delighted to see that it is still hanging on the wall of Cawsand Fish and Chips. The arcade game keeps customers entertained while they wait for their order, but the boys are able to walk straight in and start playing it; no-one bothering them as it does not interfere with the running of the shop. The game uses the new one pence piece, and they have brought a good supply with them.

David faces The Cascade and inserts his first penny into the slot at the top of the case. This sends it down and over to the right side, into an opening that partially protrudes to reveal the penny, cradled by an external trigger. It is ready to launch. He pushes it quickly with the palm of his hand, which propels the coin across the top of the playfield. The skill is in flicking the trigger just so, with the hope of getting them into one of four win holes. His first penny is unsuccessful, and it ends up in one of the columns of losing pennies. The same applies to his next six. The boys follow each coin's progress with dismay as they all join the line of other pennies now pressed against the glass. On his seventh try, he taps his coin into the win hole and it releases all the coins that had built up in the column below it. He gets his seven pennies back.

This will keep them amused for over an hour. Twenty pence worth of fun, or four shillings in old money.

~~~

'Who wants to come in for a swim?' asks Mother, tucking her hair under a pink bathing cap embellished with bright-yellow rubber flowers. Lorraine is the only taker. The beach is pebbly, not the soft sand that they are familiar with, so they hold on to each other for support as they gingerly approach the shore. The water is much calmer in this secluded cove than at Whitsands. And colder. The tiny breakers lap over their ankles. Achingly frigid. But they persevere, slowly, one short step at a time. By the time the water is gently rising and falling around them at waist height they are still holding hands, firmly clasped, raised up above the water level, their other arms outstretched for balance. Neither are ready to fully commit to the bathe. So, they just stand there, trying to acclimatize.

'Shall we do a count?' suggests Mother.

'What, like on three?'

Mother nods seriously.

'Ready?'

Lorraine takes a deep breath and exhales, blowing out through pursed lips.

'One.' Mother says.

'Two.' Both of them this time. They both pause a beat longer than they should. Three should have happened by now.

'Two and a half!' calls Mother, sending Lorraine into a fit of giggles.

'Two and three quarters!' she responds.

They look at each other, eyes wide open in exaggeration and expectation, knowing that there is no turning back after three quarters.

'Three!' they shout together. And in they go. Their shoulders are under. But only briefly.

'It's so cold!' says Lorraine, popping up.

'Ah, you'll get used to it.'

But they never did. Or, at least, they did not stay in long enough to find out if that would be true.

'Exhilarating!' says Mother as they reach the family group. 'You should try it, you lot. Lovely!'

Father glances at her over the top of his newspaper.

'It didn't look lovely,' Peter observes, a little grumpy, bored by this type of leisure, tossing small stones, aiming at a much bigger stone a few feet in front of him. It was not the sort of beach that you could play any games on. Or explore. He and Kathy had checked out a couple of rock pools, but that was it. They only have one full day left after this. It is Friday tomorrow, so he feels like he is wasting precious time away from Whitsands.

Mother quickly throws her changing robe over her head.

She made the robe herself on her sewing machine out of a large bathing towel, fashioning it into a cape of sorts, like an armless smock that reaches down below the knees. She is able to modestly dry herself, change out of her swimsuit and back into her summer dress. By the time she has swopped her swim cap for her straw hat the two young boys return to the beach, loose change jangling in the pockets of their shorts.

'How about them pasties then?' suggests the ever-hungry Mark.

At least there's that, thinks Peter.

27.
A Bonfire.

The second Friday was always the last chance for every-thing. The last charge down the cliff path to the beach. The last swim. The last low tide. The last high tide. The last game of cricket. The last game of football. The last game of badminton. The last picnic on the beach. The last scamper across the rocks. The last walk along the beach. The last leap off the flat rock. The last inspection of the boiler. The last chance to get a tan. The last sunset.

〜〜

On the final night, each year, they would have a small bonfire on the beach. Mother and Father would usually stay behind, having a quiet evening to themselves for once, while the children all head down together. For some reason, it is the only time during the fortnight that they spend time at the beach after twilight. It was dark and mysterious down there at night.

Mark is carrying two weeks' worth of daily newspapers under his arm. Lorraine has a bag full of potatoes (all pre-wrapped in foil) and a cellar of salt. Peter carries the cricket bat and ball. Kevin leads the group with a big torch – not necessary just yet, but they will need it on the way back up. There is still some light remaining, and the rising moon is bright, almost full, so they are all able to find their steps without stumbling. When they arrive at the beach, they spread out and quickly begin to gather driftwood. The sea is a long way out tonight. Dark, slaty green, mostly silent, and unfriendly. Soon a reasonable amount is collected to get the fire started. David takes charge, cupping a lit match and slowly bringing it towards a corner of scrunched up newspaper to induce a flame. It takes several attempts as the breeze knocks it out almost as soon as the match is struck. David leans in closer to the pile and this time uses three matches together for a better prospect of catching. Finally, the paper smokes encouragingly and he pokes it deeper into the centre of the pile, first with his fingers and then with a long stick, crouching as he wills it to take, poking smaller sticks into the flame, blowing on the fire gently, adding fresh sheets of bundled up paper to feed it. This is the crucial point in lighting the fire, and David is focused.

Most of the others are playing French cricket, a more

social form of the traditional game. There is only one batsman and their objective is not to be dismissed. There are no runs. In fact, the batsman must stand with his legs tight together and not move, with the bat face-on, protecting his legs. Anyone can throw the ball from the point where it lands in the sand if it has not been caught, trying to hit his legs or produce a shot that would result in a catch. Whoever gets the batsman out replaces them. The family play a version where the batsman is not allowed to turn to face the person throwing the ball, meaning they need to twist around to try and face the throw, which makes it more fun. It also makes it easier to get them out, so it keeps the game moving along. Kathy is pretty good at it, and it takes them several minutes before she pops up a catch that is taken comfortably by Peter, diving unnecessarily into the soft sand for effect. He likes to call himself 'the cat' when he plays goalie, so no one is surprised by his theatrics.

Lorraine joins David, carrying another armful of sticks and wood pieces that she has collected from the beach, as he continues to poke and prod the fire.

'Shall we put the potatoes in?' she asks her brother as she drops the load nearby.

'Not yet,' he replies with authority for one so young, 'we need to wait till we get some embers.'

They have only ever attempted to bake potatoes in the fire. No-one has ever thought to try something different, like marshmallows on sticks for instance. The fire itself is the main event and baking the potatoes was suggested almost as an after-thought. They had already eaten their tea earlier, at the usual hour, so they are not even hungry. They do it for the fun of it. It gives the fire some purpose.

As the light disappears the game of cricket is abandoned, and they all gather around the bonfire, sitting quietly, watching the flames and feeling the heat. The bonfire is the only source of light now. Lorraine is finally given permission to add the foil-wrapped potatoes to the fire. To cook through properly they should be given at least an hour, then the skins would be crisp, the interior soft. But some of the family do not have the patience, so after twenty minutes, with urgings from Mark, David drags one of the potatoes out from the centre of the fire with his stick. Mark picks it up and treats it for what it is, a hot potato, juggling it from hand to hand, willing it to cool down. Eventually he peels back the layer of foil and takes a tentative bite. Naturally, the potato is still hard, but he manages to scrape off a layer with his front teeth. It is too hot still, but he persists, even though the potato is basically raw. After another ten minutes David pulls out another one to test. It is not much different to Mark's potato, so he has the idea of putting it back in without the foil wrap, as if the barrier was what was keeping it from cooking through. All this does is burn the skin, charred now to a black cinder. He also cannot find it again in the darkness, despite the torch light. After forty-five minutes all the potatoes are retrieved from the fire, still undercooked but at least partially edible.

They gnaw on them, constantly passing around the salt cellar for each new bite. David puts his potato back in, laying it on the open foil. This also blackens quickly, just like the first one, so when he bites into it, ashes coat his teeth. But it is so dark now, the flame of the fire is almost out, that no-one notices. At least not until they get back to the cottage, when it becomes a source of great amusement. Which breaks their melancholy, because the last walk back up the cliff from the beach is the saddest of them all. This is when they begin to accept that the holiday is all but over. Just one more night's sleep. Tomorrow will be all about packing up. No time for the beach. Thoughts start turning beyond the present and their glorious fortnight at Whitsands. The first night of the holiday seemed like only yesterday.

28.

Run-Ragged, part two.

On the final morning of the holiday, during the big pack-up, amid the chaos of preparing for departure, the children are instructed to gather the clothes that they do not need anymore; their run-ragged piles – their holy socks, misshapen tees and jumpers, their ripped pants and too-small dresses, their grubby shirts, their too-far-gone underwear, their busted plimsolls and plastic sandals with broken buckles. They each bring them out to the front garden, where Father thrusts them into carrier bags. This is the first time that Peter realizes what his father is about to do. He cannot believe it.

'You're just going to throw it over the cliff?' he asks incredulously.

'Yep. It's okay, no one can see it down there, it'll all get lost in the foliage,' Father explains as he launches the first of five stuffed carrier bags. His confidence, Peter realizes, implies that he has done this before; Peter must not have been paying attention in previous years, it had never crossed his mind where the old clothes went. But what his father said was true, and as Peter follows the trajectory of the final bag it disappears from view, swallowed up by the bracken. There are no other cottages below theirs, and the cliff juts out a long way before dropping off steeply to the beach. If you looked back up from the beach towards Ferndale, that part of the cliff could not be seen, obscured by the angle. Peter shrugs, then thinks to himself, *Those sandals will probably be there forever.*

〜

They all go down for a last look at the sea. Lorraine, Kathy and David are going in, defying the reasoning that Friday was the final chance for everything. They don't bathe for very long, it is more about the opportunity than the actual swim itself. The tide is fully in, the waves are lacklustre. There is no beach available to them. As the three swimmers dry off, shivering under their towels, the rest of the family stand in a row on the pebbly edge between the bigger rocks and the sand and look out to the horizon. There is not much they can do, which actually makes it easier to leave. Although they still feel the wrench of leaving the sea as they climb back up the path for the last time, glancing back at every turn.

Mother does the final walkthrough of the cottage. Making sure the place is left as they found it.

'Back to porridge,' she announces, her Irish way of saying it was time to go back home. She locks the door behind her and puts the key back in the hiding spot under the flat stone. She walks to the front of the cottage for one last gaze out to sea, and then turns away. On reflection, they had barely done anything really, but it had been a marvelous holiday.

~~~

Without the run-ragged clothes that have been tossed over the cliff, and with just a few bags of leftover groceries, the trip back up the cliff to go home is tackled in one straight run. No need for staging and shuttling between points. The load is divided evenly between them. It is a low-energy trudge, not just because it is uphill all the way. Nor that they each have a fairly bulky, heavy load to carry. Nor that the sun is beating down on them – a gloriously sunny morning, blue sky, no clouds. They are all lost in their own thoughts as the holiday is over for another year, thinking about what is next after being able to put it out of their minds for the last week or so. Thoughts that were with them when they began the holiday, which gradually faded away as they settled into their new routines; but then, as the final weekend approached, the same thoughts started seeping back. Now, as they were beginning the ascent to the cliff top, they were each confronting them in silence.

Kevin is looking forward to the biggest change of them all.

In a couple of weeks, he will be moving out of the family home to Southampton to study Aerodynamics and Astrophysics. A new life beckons. And he is feeling pretty good about it.

Not so much disruption for the three girls. Lorraine will be in her final year of school, her A level year, while Julie is a year below her, beginning her first year of A level studies in the lower sixth form. She has just remembered that her O level results have most likely been sitting on the doormat at home for a few days, and suddenly feels a little nauseated.

Kathy will be in her O level year. She is excited to get back to studying; probably the only one of them all whom is looking forward to the transition from summer break to the school term.

Mark is supposed to start his lower sixth form, but he has been thinking to himself about dropping out and getting a job. He hates school. It has been at the back of his mind for the whole summer, only now is it coming to a head. He is going to have to tell his parents, rather than ask them. Sooner, rather than later.

Peter is about to begin his fourth year at school. His third-year review said that he was very smart, but a bit of a slacker: a criticism calculated to shame him into working harder. But it has had the opposite effect; he was actually delighted with this description and is intending to continue to coast along.

David will go into the second year. New subjects. New teachers. He is looking forward to seeing his friends again, but not much more than that. Like his two older brothers before him, he gets bored easily at school, which leads to mischievous behaviour.

He is influenced by the relentless playfulness of his oldest brother and the inherent Irish wit from his mother's side of the family. At the end of the last term, he gained notoriety during the annual school photograph. All the students and faculty were called to the rugby field, where rows of benches had been arranged to accommodate the entire body in tiers. In order to fit them all in, the photographer relied on a panoramic camera from which he would produce a long print, traditionally framed and hung proudly in the school corridor along with decades' worth of other such images. Like a wedding photographer, he exerted a lot of energy in getting everyone organized. To focus on the camera. To smile. To stand up straight, and especially to remain very still as the lens swung in an arc, building up its image on the film as it moved very slowly along the group. David had heard the rumour that it was possible to be in the picture twice. He positioned himself at one end, sitting cross-legged on the floor along with the first years. Once the lens started moving, with the photographer already concentrating ahead of the panning, urging them all to keep very still, David got up unnoticed. He sprinted behind the assembled gathering and joined it at the other end, before the camera had reached them, sitting nonchalantly in the same pose as before. He was looking forward to checking out the framed print on his first day back, to see if his audacity had paid off.

Martin is about to start a new school, joining three of his older brothers there. Those three are each moving up a year. He will be known by the teachers already, his family name going before him. He is worried that he will not be able to live up to the standards that they have set. They have all managed to stay in the top tiers of their year, and he is worried that he will be the first one in the family, boy or girl, to be assigned in one of the lower forms based on his eleven-plus score.

Father will be back at work on Monday morning. Just a day and a half for him to adjust. He thinks that he will tend to the garden on Sunday: mow the lawn, gather the produce that will have grown, pull up weeds. He will spend a full day putting it in order. A comforting transition between holiday and work.

Mother is thinking out loud with Kathy, who is just ahead of her on the path. Small-picture stuff, short-term planning.

'We could do beans on toast tonight. We'll need to pick up a loaf from the shops this afternoon, they'll all be closed tomorrow. I'll send a couple of the boys. Maybe get a chicken too for a Sunday roast. Bit of a treat.'

Father will take the rolls of film into Boots on Monday, but it will be a few weeks before all the photographs will be developed. They will be in colour this year.

The children ask him every day when he comes home from work whether he has the pictures yet. The day when he finally says that he has them is a cause for celebration, a chance for them to relive all the captured moments. Some posed. Some candid.

The one of Mother dozing on the beach, her straw hat pulled down over her eyes. The one of the three girls with Fred, feet dangling off the flat rock, sitting on bright-coloured towels, grinning at the camera and squinting against the sun. The one of Father and Cyril at the water's edge, full length, smiling, arms crossed, chests out, the vast ocean behind them. The one of the Lanes, sitting on the beach, the children distracted by their mother handing out sandwiches, Mr Lane the only one acknowledging the camera. The one of Kevin in the front garden, managing to point at the chapel on Rame Head in the distance, as if his finger is hovering directly above it. The one of Father, head tilted, drying out his ears with a beach towel. The one of the family sat on the beach, arranged in file, Mother and Father in deck chairs next to each other, the children in front of them by age, legs open to accommodate each other in a tight group.

Each one of the photographs is deemed fit for the album.

Epilogue.

This was to be the last time that all ten of them would spend a holiday together at Whitsands, or indeed anywhere.

The following summer, Kevin works on a chicken farm, a questionable improvement on the gore of his previous holiday job. He fills the feeding troughs from heavy sacks of pelleted food, cleans out the filthy cages, collects the newly laid eggs, processes and dispatches the hens as part of an assembly line, then finally plucks their feathers. All in a day's work. He sits alone at the back of the bus at the end of each shift, the stink of poultry on him too much to share. This experience briefly turns him into a vegetarian. He works through a full ten weeks to earn the extra money he will need to sustain his college lifestyle.

Lorraine works at the glove counter in Pophams, a department store in Plymouth. A rather dull appointment considering the lack of demand for gloves in the summer season. She twiddles her thumbs all day, trying to look busy.

Julie spends the entire summer serving ice cream to tourists and holidaymakers from a kiosk overlooking Plymouth Hoe. On Sundays, the nearest bus service begins three miles away, so she has to walk for almost an hour to get there.

Mark is working full-time at his entry level job as a clerical assistant in the wages department of the Naval Dockyard. A governmental Civil Service position, he would say the most exciting aspect of his time there was signing the Official Secrets Act, and that happened on his first day.

All of which made the next holiday quite comfortable for the remaining six. Kathy had her own room. The boys were happy to share the triple-bunk room. No-one needed to unfold the pull-out bed every night in the living room. They could all fit comfortably around the dining table: two on each side, one at either end. The bathroom was not always occupied. It was all far less hectic. Much quieter. Peaceful. What, they assumed, a normal family life must be like. They would never recapture that earlier time, with all ten of them together.

As the years passed, each of the children found reasons not to go back: moving away from home, summer work commitments, or, that it simply no longer appealed. When Mother and Father finally had two weeks in August at Whitsands all by themselves, it just was not the same, so they decided it was time to let it go.

~~~

Forty years later, David would return on a day trip with his wife and four grown-up sons. He fondly recounted all the stories and the places to them: the haircuts, the run-ragged clothes, all the food, the journeys in the van, the wreck, the lighthouse, the boiler, the shortcuts on the cliff path, the flat rock, the rock pools, Main Beach, the tides, ninety-nines, the games of football and cricket, French cricket, swimming in the sea, the bonfires and hot potatoes, the sloped floor in Ferndale, the gas lamps, the triple-bunk bed, that time Kathy fell out, the veranda, Kevin and his water trick, Masses at Millbrook, bullocks and farms, Cawsands, the double-decker bus rides, Mrs Bellamy, the Lanes, Fred and Cyril.

All the things.

Acknowledgements

With thanks to Kevin, Lorraine, Julie, Mark, Kathy, Pete and Dave for their collective memories and 'swing the lamp' stories.

Edited by Richard Arcus.

Cover photograph colourisation by Jordan Lloyd.

Cover and layout design by Martin Yeeles.

Special thanks to Michele, for the first-draft edits, her support and encouragement.

About the author

Martin is the second-youngest of nine children. He is a graphic designer. This is his first book. Born in Plymouth, England, he has lived in the US for nearly thirty years with his wife, Michele.